UNDER PRESSURE . . .

Tiny bubbles of sweat climbed up the sides of Hack's neck, growing colder as they went. The tips of his ears froze into thin curves of ice. His lungs filled with snow, ballooning, prying his ribs outward against the cells of his pressure suit. Hack jigged and jagged, throwing the plane back and forth as he tried desperately to avoid the SAMs.

The sharp maneuvers sent gravity crushing against his body. Even as his g suit worked furiously to ward off the pressure, Hack's world narrowed to a pinprick of brown and blue, surrounded by a circle of black. He heard nothing, he felt nothing. He knew his fingers were curled hard around the stick only because he saw them there . . .

Don't miss the previous HOGS novels!

HOGS

GOING DEEP

HOG DOWN

FORT APACHE

SNAKE EATERS

TARGET: SADDAM

HOGS #6
DEATH WISH

JAMES FERRO

BERKLEY BOOKS, NEW YORK

HOGS: DEATH WISH

A Berkley Book / published by arrangement with the author

PRINTING HISTORY
Berkley edition / January 2002

Visit our website at
www.penguinputnam.com

ISBN: 0-425-18306-8

BERKLEY®
Berkley Books are published by The Berkley Publishing Group, a division of Penguin Putnam Inc., 375 Hudson Street, New York, New York 10014.
BERKLEY and the "B" design are trademarks belonging to Penguin Putnam Inc.

PRINTED IN THE UNITED STATES OF AMERICA

10 9 8 7 6 5 4 3 2 1

Prologue

Standing watch one afternoon in their trench a few yards from the Iraqi border, Private Smith and Private Jones began discussing aesthetics.

Or more particularly, how shitfully ugly the desert was.

The conversation soon turned to a comparison of the ugliest things they had ever seen.

"The back end of a seventies Buick," said Jones.

"Mary Broward's face," said Smith.

"Things, things," said Jones, trying to rein in the discussion.

"She *was* a thing."

"If you're includin' stuff like that," Jones sniped, "Sergeant Porky's rear end."

"You saw Porky's butt?" asked Smith.

Jones's response was drowned out by the whiz and explosion of a trio of Iraqi shells landing uncomfortably close to their sandbags. It was the third attack of the afternoon, and by far the most accurate. Geysers of dirt burst over their trench, covering their prone backs with grit. The ground shook as the pounding continued, and it quickly became clear that this time the Iraqis were serious about what they were doing—the rain of explosives started a slow but steady walk toward the privates, the enemy homing in on their position.

"Mayday, Mayday," screamed Smith, grabbing for the com pack that connected them with HQ. "Shit, incoming. We're taking serious incoming."

"Let's get the hell out of here," shouted Jones, grabbing his buddy. Just as they rose, a blast pushed them facedown in the sand.

"Pray! Pray!" yelped Smith.

As Jones started to carry out his friend's suggestion, a fresh sound filled the air, a hum that managed to carry over the steady roar of the steadily approaching explosions. The hum became a roar, then a piercing whine and a loud metallic hush, the sound a steel bar might make if it were being beaten back into molten ore. The ground reverberated with the hiss of a thousand volcanoes. The sky flashed with lightning, and both men felt their ears pop.

Then, silence.

Smith and Jones managed to rub the sand out of their faces and look skyward just in time to see their saviors circling above: a pair of U.S. Air Force A-10A Thunderbolt II attack planes, better known as Warthogs, or simply Hogs. The A-10's had flattened the enemy artillery with a strong but simple dose of Maverick AGM-65 air-to-ground missiles. The dark-hulled beasts tipped their ungainly wings back and forth in greeting, then flew off.

"Now that's fuckin' ugly," said Jones.

"Ugly, fuckin' ugly," agreed Smith. "How the hell do they fly?"

"Damned if I know. Too ugly to land, I guess."

"I could kiss 'em."

"Me too."

"Saved my butt," said Jones.

"Now that's ugly."

"Not half as ugly as yours."

"Not half as ugly as theirs." Smith thumbed back toward the planes.

"Damn ugly."

"Most beautiful fuckin' ugly I ever saw."

"Damn straight."

PART ONE

DRIVERS

1

It briefed damn easy: Head exactly north four miles off the last way-marker, dive below the cloud cover, plink the tanks.

But in the air, falling through thick clouds at five thousand feet, just finding the Iraqi T-54 tanks was an accomplishment.

Or would be. Major Horace Gordon Preston, better known as "Hack," clenched his back teeth and pushed harder on the stick, urging the nose of his A-10A Thunderbolt II "Warthog" downward. The Hog grunted, her angle of attack slicing through forty-five degrees as she finally broke through the thick deck of clouds. Unblemished yellow sand spread out before her, oblivious to the war. The targeting cue in the plane's heads-up display ghosted white and empty over the dirt as Hack hunted for the vehicles.

They were supposed to be dug into a revetment on the southwestern end of Kill Box Alpha Echo Five. He had the right place, and it was unlikely that the Iraqis would have moved the tanks this early in the morning. They had to be here somewhere.

He was going to nail them the second he saw them. A pair of Maverick AGM-65B electro-optical magnifaction air-to-ground missiles hung on his wings, balanced by four Mark-20 Rockeye II cluster-bombs. The Mavericks would be fired first; he'd then close on whatever was left of the target and pop the Rockeyes.

Assuming he found something to pop them on.

"Yo, Devil One, you got our cupcakes yet?"

"One. Negative," snapped Hack, answering his wing mate, Captain Thomas "Shotgun" O'Rourke.

"Try nine o'clock, four miles."

Hack glanced to the northwest. A brown smudge sat in the distance there, too far away for him to make out. Still, it was something; he angled his wings and turned in that direction, leveling out of his dive. The nine-inch television screen at the right side of his cockpit control panel fed video from the optical head in the missile on his port wing: a perfect gray-scale image of undulating sand.

Preston glued his eyes to the attitude indicator in the middle of the dash, momentarily worrying that he'd lost his sense of where he was. He was low and out of position for an attack, and realized he should tell Shotgun to take the lead.

But that would have felt too much like giving up.

I'm only flying a Hog, he reminded himself. I can plink tanks with my eyes closed.

Three or four years ago, that might have been true. He was a high-time A-10 driver then, with tons of experience in Europe. But he hated slogging around in the slow-moving, low-flying planes. Flying them was about as glamorous as going to the prom with your mom's grandmother, and not half as good for your career. Finally, his Washington connections came through with better gigs, transferring him briefly to the Pentagon before finally sliding him into an F-15C wing. He came to the Gulf with the fast movers, flying as a section leader; only a few days ago he'd nailed a MiG in aerial combat over Iraq.

Within twenty-four hours—hell, within four—he was transferred to Devil Squadron, back out of the fast lane, back into Mom's grandmom's Model T.

The general who came through with the billet advertised it as a command move, the chance to lead a squadron, admittedly one of Hack's most cherished goals. He hadn't told him it was with A-10's until it was too late. Nor was it a real command—he was only the squadron's director of operations or DO, second in line behind the commander.

The way Hack was flying today, he was lucky someone didn't bust him back to lieutenant. He needed more altitude to make the attack work. Still not entirely confident that the smudge was anything but a smudge, he began a tight bank, intending to spiral upward like a hawk as he proceeded.

The A-10 groaned. Never particularly adept at climbing, the plane labored with a full load tied to her wings.

"Come on," he told the plane.

"Yo, Hack, you got 'em?" asked Shotgun.

"I'm not sure that's our target."

Preston could practically hear Shotgun snickering through the static. He came through his bank and pushed his wings level, now dead on for the dark brown clumps. Maybe tanks, maybe not—the video screen was a blurry mess.

Could be a pair of T-54's buried in the sand. Then again, it could be an *I Love Lucy* episode.

A few stray clouds wisped in to further obstruct his vision. Hack cursed at the gray fingers, flipping back and forth between the two magnification cones offered by the missile gear in a vain hope that it would magically help him find the tanks.

He needed to find the damn things. Partly because he wanted to prove to Shotgun and the rest of the squadron that he did really and truly have the right stuff. And partly because he wanted to prove it to himself.

Not that he should need to. But somehow the fuzzy picture in the small targeting screen and the rust in his Hog-flying chops negated everything.

Hack checked his fuel and then his paper map as he legged further north. He pushed the air through his lungs slowly, telling himself to calm down.

Below the map and the mission notes, taped to the last page of the knee board, were three pieces of paper. He flipped the sheets up and looked at them now, talismans that never failed him.

One was a Gary Larson cartoon about scientists and bugs. He looked at it and laughed.

The second was a Biblical quotation from Ecclesiastes, reminding him that "wisdom exceedeth folly."

And the last was the most important, a motto he'd heard from his father since he was seven or eight years old:

"Do your best."

All he could do. He blew another wad of air into his face mask and put his eyes back out into the desert, trying to will some detail out of the shifting sands. The smudge had worked itself into a dark brown snake on the ground.

Not a tank. Something, but not a tank.

Hack sighed—might just as well let Shotgun take a turn; he was used to looking at things on the ground, and maybe his eyes were even better. But as Preston lifted his finger to click on the mike, the transmission from another flight ran over the frequency. Waiting for it to clear, he saw a gray lollipop just beyond the snake. Then another and another and another.

"Thank you, God, oh, thank you," he said, looking over and dialing the Maverick's targeting cursor onto the first T-54.

"You say something, Major?" asked Shotgun.

"Have three, no, four tanks dug in beyond that smudge," said Hack as he coaxed the pipper home. "Stand by."

"Story of my life," said Shotgun. "Yeah, I got them. Your butt's clear. Ooo, look at that. Track from a flak gun real artistic, kind of like a snake on acid. Zeus on the right of the target area. Two of 'em. Firing!"

As if they'd heard his wing mate's warning, the four-barreled antiaircraft guns sent a stream of lead into the air.

They were firing at extreme range and without the help of their radar, but even if they'd been in his face, Hack wouldn't have paid any attention—he wanted the damn tanks.

His first Maverick slid off her rail with a thunk, the rocket engine taking a second before bursting into action. By that time Hack had already steadied the crosshairs on a second tank. One hundred and twenty-five pounds of explosive dutifully took its cue as he depressed the trigger, launching from the Hog on what would be a fast, slightly arced, trip to its target. Hack jerked his head back to the windscreen, belatedly realizing he was flying toward the antiaircraft fire. Well-aimed or not, the 23mm slugs could still make nasty holes in anything they hit. He jerked the plane sharply to his right, narrowly avoiding the furious lead roiling the air.

2

As soon as Hack cleared to his right, Shotgun dished off his two Mavericks, targeting the pair of four-barreled 23mm antiaircraft guns that were sending a fury of shells at his flight leader.

"What I'm talking about," Shotgun told the missiles as they sped toward their destinations. "What I'm talking about is nobody fires on a Hog and gets away with it. Go shoot at an F-15 or something. Better yet, aim for a MiG."

Never one to waste a motion, Shotgun nudged his stick ever so slightly to the left, lining up to drop his cluster-bombs on the buried tanks. In the fraternity of Hog drivers, Shotgun stood apart. He was a wingman's wingman, always checking somebody's six, always ready to smoke any son of a bitch with the bad manners to attack his lead. But he did have his quirks—he never entered combat without a full store of candy in his flight suit, and never dropped a bomb without an appropriate sound track.

"Sweet Child o' Mine" qualified as appropriate, if you skipped the mushy parts.

As W. Axl Rose prayed for thunder, Shotgun tipped into a swoop toward the targets, planning to drop his Redeye cluster-bombs in two salvos. In the meantime, Hack's first Maverick hit its target, the nose of the flying bomb sending a small gray-black geyser into the air.

No flames, no satisfying pop of the turret.

"Decoy," said Shotgun. "Son of a bitch."

3

Hack rarely cursed, but he found it nearly impossible not to as he swung back toward the target area. Shotgun might or might not be right about the tanks being decoys—hazy smoke now covered the target area, making it impossible to tell whether the T-54's had been made of metal or papier-mâché. Flames shot up from one of the antiaircraft guns his wing mate had hit; black fingers erupted in crimson before closing back into a fist and disappearing. Hack turned on his wing, edging north, still trying to figure out what the hell he was seeing on the ground.

In an F-15, everything was laid out for you. AWACS caught the threat miles and miles away, fed you a vector. The APG-70 multimode, pulse-Doppler radar sifted through the air, caught the bandit eighty miles away, hiding in the weeds. You closed, selected your weapon. Push button, push button—two Sparrows up and at 'em. The MiG was dead meat before it even knew you were there.

Push button, push button.

If the MiG got through the net, things could get dicey. But that was good in a way—you scanned the sky, saw a glint off a cockpit glass, came up with your solution, applied it. You might even tangle mano a mano, cannons blazing away.

But this—this was like trying to ride a bicycle on a highway in a sandstorm. You were looking at the ground, for christsakes, not the sky.

The desert blurred. He shifted in the ejection seat, leaning up to get a better view; his elbow slapped hard against the left panel, pinging his funny bone.

Stinking A-10.

Hack pulled through a bank of clouds and ducked lower, jerking the stick hard enough to feel the g's slam him in the chest. He'd been out of sorts his first few times in the Eagle cockpit, out of whack again when he'd come over here for his first combat patrols, unsettled even the day he nailed his Iraqi. There were no natural pilots, or if there were, he didn't know any and he certainly wasn't one of them. There were guys who worked at it hard, set their marks, and hit them. You learned to keep the bile in your stomach, slow your breathing, take your time—but not too much time.

Do your best.

"I'm thinking we get rid of our cluster-bombs and maybe have a go with the guns on the cracker box." Shotgun's transmission took him by surprise.

"Come again?" Hack asked.

"Cracker box, make that a box of Good & Plenty, two o'clock on your bow, three, oh, maybe four miles off. Looks like the candy's spilling out of it. See?"

Hack stared for at least thirty seconds before finally spotting the building. Shotgun had incredible eyes.

"How come everything is food to you, Shotgun?" Hack asked, nudging his stick.

"Could be I'm hungry," replied his wing mate.

Shotgun's "candy" looked suspiciously like howitzer shells. Their frag—slang for the "fragment" of the daily Air Tasking Order pertaining to them—allowed them to hit any secondary target in the kill box once the tanks were nailed. Still, Hack contacted the ABCCC controller circling to the south in a C-130 to alert him to the situation, in effect asking if they were needed elsewhere. Important cogs in the machinery of war, the ATO and the ABCCC (airborne command and control center) allowed the Allies to coordinate hundreds of strikes every day, giving them both a game plan and a way to freelance around it. Dropping ordnance was one thing; putting explosives where they would do the most good was another. Coordination was especially important this close to Kuwait, where there were thousands of targets and almost as many aircraft.

The controller told them the building was a hospital and off-limits.

"No way that's a fucking hospital," said Shotgun. "I'm looking at ammo for twenty fucking guns. Shit, look in the shadow there. See the tarp? Fuck. Four artillery pieces, probably a shitload more. Fuck. Fuck this hospital shit."

Hack waited for O'Rourke's curses to subside, then gave the ABCCC controller another shot. But he wasn't buying.

"Devil One, we'll have a FAC check it out on the coordinates you supplied," said the controller finally. "I have a target for you."

Hack's fingers fumbled his wax pencil, and he had to dig into his speed-suit pocket for the backup. He retrieved it just as the controller began the brief setting out an armored vehicle depot as the new target. Hack scrawled the coordinates on the Persipex canopy, then double-checked them against his paper map, orienting himself. The target was to the east, a stretch for their fuel.

Doable, though.

Shotgun continued to grumbled about the ersatz hospital, even after they changed course.

"Hospital my ass."

Hack tried coordinating the numbers against his map, but lost track of where he was for a moment, thrown a bit by the INS. You could get distracted easily in combat, no matter what you were flying. He had to keep his head clear.

The opposite seemed true for Shotgun. "I've seen more convincing hospitals in comic books," he railed.

"O'Rourke, shut the hell up and watch my six," barked Preston finally.

"What I'm talking about."

This time, there was no difficulty seeing the target. It had been bombed in the past hour or so; smoke curled from the remains of buildings or bunkers at the north and south ends of what looked like a large parking lot. Roughly two dozen vehicles were parked in almost perfect rows at a right angle to the buildings. Beyond them were mounds of dirt—probably more vehicles dug into the sand. Whatever air defenses the Iraqis had mounted had been eradicated in the earlier strike.

A flight of F-16 Vipers cut overhead as Hack turned to line up his bombing run. At least five thousand feet separated him from the nearest plane, but it still felt like he was getting his hair cut. He hadn't known about the flight, which was en route to another target; Hack fought against an impulse to bawl them out or bawl the controller out for not warning him that they were nearby.

Do your best, he reminded himself as he nudged tentatively into the bombing run. The A-10A's relatively primitive bombsight slid slowly toward the row of vehicles as he dropped through nine thousand feet. They were small brown sticks, tiny twigs left in the dirt by a kid who'd gone home for supper.

Hack's heart thumped loudly in his throat, choking off his breath. He began to worry that he was going to be too low before the crosshairs found their target, then realized he'd begun his glide a bit too late; he was in danger of overshooting the vehicles. He pushed his stick, increasing his angle of attack. The cursor jumped onto a pair of fat sticks and he pickled.

Wings now clean except for the Sidewinders and ECM pod, the Hog fluttered slightly, urging her pilot to recover to the right as planned. But Hack's attention stayed focused on the ground in front of him, the twigs steadily growing to thick branches. The bark roughened and indentations appeared. They were armored personnel carriers, all set out in a line. He could see hatches and machine guns, sloped ports. He stared at them as they grew, watching with fascination as they became more and more real, yet remained the playthings of a kid.

Finally he pulled his stick back, belatedly realizing he'd flown so close to the ground that the exploding bomblets might very well clip his wings. He reached for the throttle, slamming the Hog into overdrive, ducking his body with the plane as he tried desperately to push her off to the south.

It was only as the Hog began to recover that Hack realized he hadn't remembered to correct for the wind before dropping his bombs.

Had they missed?

As he twisted his head back to get a look, Shotgun's garbled voice jangled his ears. He started to ask his wing mate to repeat, then realized what the words meant.

Someone on the ground had fired a shoulder-launched SAM at Hack's tailpipe.

4

Shotgun repeated his warning, then stepped hard on his
rudder pedal, twisting his A-10A in the air. The ants that
had emerged from the burned-out bunker were fat and
pretty in his screen—no way could he waste a shot like
this, even if there were missiles in the air. He kissed his last
cluster-bombs good-bye, then tossed a parcel of decoy
flares off for luck, tucking the Hog into a roll.

He swirled almost backward in the air, goosing more
flares off before finally pushing Devil Two level in the opposite direction from the one he'd taken for the attack. If
either of the SA-7's that had been launched were aimed at
him, his zigging maneuvers had tied their primitive heat
seekers in knots.

Probably.

Something detonated in the air about a half-mile north
of him. Immediately above the explosion but a good mile
beyond it, Devil One crossed to the west.

Assured that his wing mate hadn't been hit, Shotgun

pulled his plane over his shoulder, flailing back at the armored depot to share his feelings at being fired on.

"I'm a touchy-feely kind of guy," he explained as Iraqis scattered below. "So let me just hug you close."

The 30mm Avenger cannon began growling below his feet. Nearly the size of the '59 Caddy Shotgun had on blocks back home, the Gatling's seven barrels sped around furiously. High-explosive and uranium armor-piercing shells were fed into the barrels by a pair of hydraulic motors, only to be dispensed by the Gat with furious relish. The recoil from the gun literally held the Hog in the air as the pilot worked the stream of bullets through the top armor of three APCs.

As smoke and debris filled the air before him, Shotgun pushed the Hog to the right, leaning against the stick to fight off a sudden tsunami of turbulence. He let off the trigger as he came to the end of the row, pushing away now at only seven hundred feet, close enough for some of the crazy ragheads on his left to actually take aim with their Kalashnikovs. The assault rifles' 7.62mm bullets were useless against the titanium steel surrounding the Hog's cockpit, and it would take more than a hundred of them to seriously threaten the honeycombed wings with their fire-retardant inserts protecting the fuel tanks.

Still, it was the thought that counted.

"I admire the hell out of you," said Shotgun. Then he turned back to nail the SOBs. "Let me show you what a real gun can do," he said as he zipped back for the attack, the Iraqis diving on the ground. "Do the words thirty-millimeter cannon mean anything to you? How about u-rain-ee-um?"

5

Tiny bubbles of sweat climbed up the sides of Hack's neck, growing colder as they went. The tips of his ears froze into thin curves of ice. His lungs filled with snow, ballooning, prying his ribs outward against the cells of his pressure suit. Hack jigged and jagged, throwing the plane back and forth as he tried desperately to avoid the SAMs.

The sharp maneuvers sent gravity crushing against his body. Even as his g suit worked furiously to ward off the pressure, Hack's world narrowed to a pinprick of brown and blue, surrounded by a circle of black. He heard nothing, he felt nothing. He knew his fingers were curled hard around the stick only because he saw them there.

The plane was going where he didn't want it to.

He pulled back on the stick, struggling to clear his head and keep himself airborne. The black circle began to retreat. The wings lifted suddenly, air pushing the plane upward. Something rumbled against the rudders.

I'm hit, he thought. Damn, I'm going in.

His lungs had a thousand sharp points, digging into the soft tissue around them.

Do your best.

The plane's shudder ceased. He eased back, leveling off.

He was free. The missile that had been chasing him had given up, exploding a few yards behind as it reached the end of its range.

Or maybe he'd just imagined it all in his panic. Maybe the g's rushing against his body had temporarily knocked him senseless, made him hallucinate. Perhaps the rush of his heart had exaggerated the danger.

It didn't matter. He was free, alive, unscathed, or at least not seriously wounded.

As deliberately as he could manage, Hack took stock of himself and his position. He was about three miles south of the target area, now clearly marked by black smoke. Open desert lay below and directly south. He was at five thousand feet, climbing very slightly, moving at just over 350 knots, a fair clip for a Hog.

Fuel—low, but not desperate.

He hadn't been hit. He'd panicked, though, if only for half a minute. The cowl of blackness had scared him shitless.

Worse.

Where the hell was Shotgun?

"Devil Two," he said over the squadron frequency. "Lost airman. Shotgun?"

"Yo," responded his wing mate.

"Where the hell are you?"

"I'm just north of Saddam's used-car parking lot, helping them put up the going-out-of-business sign."

"Where the hell are you?" Hack repeated.

"Relax, Devil Leader," said O'Rourke. "I got you. Hold your horses and I'll be on your butt. We're clean."

"What do you mean, we're clean?"

"I mean, the only thing we have to worry about is running into some of those pointy-nose types on their way to mop up."

"What are you screwing around for? Check your fuel. Come on. Didn't you get a bingo?"

Shotgun didn't answer, which was just fine with Hack. He turned southward to intersect the original course back to King Khalid, where they would refuel before heading back to the Home Drome at King Fahd.

Dark curls of black wool filled the eastern horizon. Saddam had set the Kuwait oil fields on fire and released thousands, maybe millions, of gallons of oil into the Gulf, doing to the environment what he had done to Kuwait.

"Got your back," said Shotgun, announcing that he had caught up and was now in combat trail, roughly a mile offset behind Hack's tail. "How 'bout we find a tanker instead of going into Khalid? Their coffee sucks."

"Can it."

"Man, you're being bitchy. What happened? That SA-7 get your underwear dirty?"

This time, Hack was the one who didn't reply.

6

Lieutenant Colonel Michael "Skull" Knowlington lowered his head toward the desktop, stretching his neck and shoulder muscles until he could feel the strain in the middle of his back. Then he rolled his head around slowly, trying to keep his shoulders relaxed as he completed each revolution. With the sixth turn he started back in the other direction, counterclockwise, moving his head as slowly as he could manage. Six more times and he put his chin on his chest, covering his face with his hands, fingers massaging his temples. Then he dropped his arms and sat upright in the chair, breathing slowly.

Though dissipated, his headache had not quite disappeared. The throb was familiar and low-grade, potentially vanquishable by one of several additional therapies, including what Skull called "the oxygen cure," breathing pure oxygen through his pilot's face mask. But there were only two sure cures: One was time, the other a drink.

Or perhaps they were the same, for wasn't he destined to drink again, again and again and again, sooner or later?

Knowlington had been sober for twenty-three days before last night. Then, on the ground at KKMC, waiting for his umpteenth debriefing, someone had stuck a beer in his hand and he'd slipped down a long, familiar hole.

Wrong.

No one made him drink the beer. He didn't slip, he went willingly. He took the beer and drank it, then got another and another.

There were extenuating circumstances. He'd gotten back from a hellacious sortie north, fighting the odds to help rescue one of his pilots, one of his kids. BJ Dixon had volunteered as a forward ground-attack controller, helping a Delta team spot Scuds deep in Iraq territory. Dixon—who was, or at least ought to be, sleeping in his quarters in nearby Tent City—had saved the life of one of the Delta boys, but gotten separated from them in the process. Devil Squadron had found him and brought him home.

As squadron commander, Knowlington had felt responsible for the kid, and gone along personally to snatch him. Everything had gone well—too damn well, which was the problem. He'd let his guard down.

Liar!

He'd wished for it. He'd known what was happening. The tingle in his mouth, the roar in his head—he knew what he was doing.

Just a few beers.

Exactly how long had he been sober? Two weeks? Three? He couldn't even remember now.

Yesterday he could have counted the minutes.

Michael Knowlington pushed back in his office chair, staring at the blank wall of his trailer headquarters.

God, he wanted a drink.

It would take him ten minutes, fifteen tops, to walk over to the Depot, an illegal "club" located just off the base property. A few slugs of Jack Daniel's and he'd be back on his feet.

He wasn't fit to command the squadron. He had to resign.

Skull turned toward the door as someone knocked. He waited a moment before saying anything, though he had already recognized the knuckles tapping against the frame.

Maybe because of that.

"Come," he said.

Chief Master Sergeant Allen Clyston pushed into the small office like a bear inspecting a new cave. Clyston was the squadron's first sergeant—and much, much more. He personally oversaw the maintenance of Devil Squadron's twelve Hogs. In the squadron's stripped-down organization chart, every enlisted arrow pointed to him. He was Knowlington's capo di capo, the colonel's right arm—and left, and legs, his eyes and ears. Clyston was the last of a veritable mafia of enlisted men who had helped Knowlington through half-a-dozen commands and assignments stretching back to the waning days of Vietnam. He knew Skull before he was ever called Skull; few people in the Air Force could say that.

"Allen."

"Colonel." Clyston groaned as he slipped onto the metal chair across from Knowlington's desk. "Ought to let me find you a real chair," offered the sergeant, whose procurement network rivaled the GSA's and was infinitely more efficient.

"Don't want visitors getting too comfortable." Knowlington tried smiling, realized how forced it must seem.

"I hear ya." The sergeant folded his arms around his chest, leaning back in the chair so his gray-speckled head touched the wall. "Got a problem I thought you could help with."

"Fire away."

"Got a fix for the INS units," said Clyston, referring to the gear that helped the A-10A's navigate. Though a basic piece of equipment, the gear was notoriously unreliable, needing constant readjustment. "Kind of a work-around-upgrade thing, but we need a pair of special diodes I can't seem to get through the usual sources." Clyston reached into his pocket for a piece of paper. "Becky Rosen says she can give them a five-year, sixty-thousand-mile warranty if she gets this stuff."

Skull's head throbbed at the mention of Sergeant Rosen. She was a damn good worker and smarter than hell, but she had caused Skull nothing but trouble. She had a way of pissing off half the officers who crossed her path. The rest made passes at her—not her fault certainly, but her way of dealing with them fell somewhat outside the parameters of the Military Code of Conduct.

Worse, she'd recently joined Delta Force in an unauthorized foray across the border to help the Army retrieve a battered helicopter. A good number of butts were hanging in the wind because a woman had gone over enemy lines.

Not that she hadn't done a kick-ass job and probably single-handedly saved the operation.

"Your channels can't get this stuff?" Skull asked Clyston, trying to make sense of the specifications.

"My channels are military," said Clyston. "Turns out those are pretty rare little circuits. Rosen claims she can adapt them to regulate the voltage and then use that to feed back against the errors. Has a little card designed and everything, neat as a pin. She's a whip, I'm telling you."

"It'll work?"

"She says so, if we can find the parts." Clyston shrugged. "You know somebody at G.E., right? They probably have something like that. Or they'd get us onto someone. Maybe a supplier of theirs or something. That G.E. guy now—Rogers, right?"

No, not Rogers. Jeff Roberts, who'd flown Phantoms with Skull out in California. Some sort of senior vice president at the company. Probably didn't know shit about electronics, but he'd love this. Roberts had always talked big about finding ways around the brass, military and otherwise.

Skull did know a Rogers, though. Had known.

Captain Slammin' Sammy Rogers had gone out over Vietnam, ended up a POW. Supposedly, he'd been at Son

Tay with a bunch of other guys shortly before the raid there in '70. Knowlington had led one of the support packages, flying a Phantom.

Volunteered, and helped with the planning. He would have gone in the helicopters if they'd let him.

The raid came up empty; Rogers never came home.

"Jeff Roberts," said Skull.

"Captain Roberts," said Clyston.

"I think he went out as a lieutenant colonel," said Skull.

Clyston's left shoulder edged up slightly in a shrug. "Pretty much a captain's attitude, though. Stays with you."

"Oh? That's a new theory."

"F no," said Clyston. He smiled. "Guy has a rank stays with him for life, whatever the stripes say. Or what have you."

"What rank am I?"

"Oh, a colonel. Definitely. Not full of shit enough to be a general. No offense." Clyston's mouth slid slowly into a smile.

The capo hadn't come here to give him the parts list. He must know about the drinking. The reference to Roberts— a subtle hint that he ought to resign?

Clyston could be very subtle. But he was also pretty straight. Very straight.

Skull folded the piece of paper and put it down on his desk. "You got something you want to say, Allen?"

"Huh? Not me. You?"

A ton of things. Angry things: How dare a sergeant hint that a colonel hang it up. A stinking decorated pilot with three confirmed air kills, three more probables, well over a hundred combat sorties, medals up the wazoo, friends in all the right places. What gave some sergeant—who'd never had his fat ass graze an enemy's gunsight, by the way—the right, the audacity to hint that he was over the hill?

Calmer things: gratitude for pulling the men together maybe a million times, for making planes whole, for moving heaven and earth to keep the squadron flying.

Other things: sadness over people like Rogers who

hadn't made it back, frustration over the delays and screw-
ups and the human factors, anger at the inevitable fatigue
and nerves. Rage that they were both growing so damn old,
that after all these years, after all they knew, they had to
keep sending kids to places where they could die.

But words were not things that came easily to Skull.
There were too many, and no way of prioritizing them—no
checklist to follow, no IP to start your attack from. Much
easier to stay silent—and so he did.

"Saddam's taking a poundin'," said Clyston finally.

"Hope so," agreed the colonel.

"How much longer, you figure?"

"That's a hard game to play," said Knowlington. He
thought of all the times he'd played it before—'Nam
mostly, ancient history, but he'd also had a squadron during Grenada, and one that just missed a mission in Panama.
Then there were the alerts, probably a thousand of them.

They were silent a moment.

"You sure nothing's bothering you, Sergeant?" Knowlington asked.

"Gettin' old, is all," said Clyston. He smiled, but it
wasn't the smile from before, not his usual ain't-this-a-
pile-of-shit smile. Allen definitely wanted to say something, his eyes hunting the office to find an opening. But
before they could settle on anything, there was another
knock on the door.

Skull glanced at Clyston, then said, "Come."

Captain Bristol Wong, an intel and covert ops specialist
Knowlington had "borrowed" from the Pentagon, pushed
open the door.

"Colonel, Captain Hawkins and Sir Peter Paddington
would like a word," announced Wong.

His voice seemed more high-strung than usual, possibly
because of the thick bandage wrapped around his chest beneath his uniform. A dark patch of skin on his face covered
a fractured cheekbone, and there were several burns along
his hairline, all souvenirs from his recent trip north to save
Dixon. He'd also dislocated his shoulder, though it had

been placed back in its socket by a burly pararescuer on the ride home.

Wong had shrugged off the injuries, claiming he'd been hurt worse trying to grab the last seat on the shuttle between Boston and D.C.

"Tell them to come in," said Skull.

"With all due respect," said Wong, nodding at Clyston, "this would be a code-word classified discussion, strictly need-to-know."

"I doubt you could fart on this base without Sergeant Clyston catching a whiff," said Skull.

The welt on Wong's cheekbone turned dark purple.

Clyston got up. "I was just leaving," said the sergeant. "Appreciate it if you get those doodads, Colonel. Let me know."

Clyston nodded to Wong, then left the office, shuffling into the hall as nonchalantly as he had entered.

Skull pushed his chair back against the desk, making room for the other men as they came in. Hawkins was a Delta Force captain who had worked with Devil Squadron before and had helped rescue Dixon. Paddington's exact status wasn't clear. He apparently served with the British MI-6 intelligence agency and worked for one of the British commands. He was an expert on Saddam Hussein and the Iraqi command structure, and seemed to fill a role as a liaison with the British Special Air Service. The SAS commandos were working north of the border spotting Scuds, scouting troop locations, and sabotaging enemy installations. Sir Peter had been involved in a failed plot to assassinate Saddam that the Hogs were in on, helping set the time and place. He flitted freely around Saudi Arabia, but his rank and role in the Allied war effort were far from obvious.

What was obvious was the stench of gin emanating from his breath, so strong that it threatened to turn Knowlington's stomach.

"Captain, good to see you again," Knowlington told Hawkins. He'd first met Hawkins two months before, planning a clandestine operation known as Fort Apache.

"Thanks." Hawkins flexed his shoulders, a linebacker waiting to blitz. "We appreciated your help on that bug-out."

"My men did that on their own," Skull said. "Right place, right time."

"Yes, sir." Hawkins sat down in the chair.

"Paddington." Skull frowned in the British agent's direction, then looked at Wong. "So?"

"The British command desires our assistance," said the captain.

"Not precisely, Bristol," said Paddington. He twisted the cuff of his blue wool blazer, as if adjusting a watch.

"Well, what is precise?" Knowlington said to the Brit, trying hard not to spit the words.

"To be precise, Colonel, SAS finds itself shorthanded for an important mission. Delta has been enlisted, and air support is desired. You have worked with Captain Hawkins before, so naturally your unit was mentioned. The target is somewhat south of As-Samawah."

" 'Somewhat south' meaning how far exactly?" said Skull.

"Not that far," answered Hawkins. The Delta Force captain clearly had little use for Paddington, and even less tolerance for BS, or Paddington's circuitous route to the point. "It's damn close to the Euphrates. No bullshit, Colonel. Serious Indian country. That's why we need Hogs with us. Delta's going to lead the mission," added Hawkins. He put up his hand to keep Paddington from interrupting. "At least this assault. According to the latest intelligence, the target has a few Zeus guns for air defenses and nothing else, but we're thinking that may change. Old airstrip, couple of buildings; it was used briefly during the Iran-Iraq war, hit by Iranian missiles, and then abandoned. Some troops there now but no planes. The Brits want to check it out. Sir Peter's here to give us the layout and report back to the general, if it's a go."

Paddington cleared his throat ostentatiously.

"You're looking for Scuds?" asked Knowlington.

"No," said Hawkins. "SAS lost two commandos. There's a chance they're being held there."

"A small chance," said Paddington. "Nonetheless, it cannot be dismissed." He touched his hand to the side of his sport coat; it occurred to Skull there must be a flask there.

If the bastard took out the flask, Skull would throttle him.

Why did Paddington's drinking bother him? The man was just a drunk, like him.

"Two other operations are planned at higher-probability sites," said Wong. "SAS is conducting them itself, with RAF support. Captain Hawkins will lead a small team of Delta and SAS men on this operation. The A-10's would strike a total of six ZSU-23-4's at the target, then remain for any necessary support during the duration of the operation."

Paddington's nose seemed to float above the room. "The operation must be surgical, precise, and brief."

"No shit," muttered Hawkins.

Skull smiled at the Delta captain. "How many planes?"

"Two, at a minimum. They clear out the antiaircraft guns, then mop up if necessary. We're in and out in an hour, no more."

"Four planes would be better," said Wong, "since there is a possibility of additional defenses being moved into position. There has been considerable radio traffic, and several Iraqi units are in the general vicinity."

Knowlington reached to his desk and opened the single drawer, taking out a large Michelin paper map of Iraq that he'd gotten in the States before deploying. As-Samawah was about midway between Baghdad and Kuwait, right on the Euphrates. If the scale at the bottom of the map was to be believed, it lay about 175 miles north of the Saudi border.

A long ride over nasty real estate.

"Can you sketch out the defenses for me, Wong?" he asked.

The captain leaned over the map. "From memory," said

the intel officer, posting a disclaimer, "there would be triple-A all along this approach that must be avoided. The Republican Guard facilities closer to the border have been mostly neutralized, but even so must be respected. An SA-6 battery is believed to lie somewhere north of the base, but has not been definitively located; its radar has never been activated so far as is known. Additionally, Humint sources have rumored several Roland batteries in this general vicinity, but again, no radars or other hard indications have been recorded. Even if they do exist, the most serious obstacle would be an SA-2 site here, twelve miles south of the base. Its radar covers nearly the entire approach. It has operated intermittently, for only a few moments at a time, undoubtedly to avoid targeting from a HARM-equipped SAM killer. Perhaps it is working with human spotters. There is also a possibility that it is not actually functional, as the intercepts have never been strong or of long duration. Nonetheless, it can be avoided if the A-10's travel a very precise path, breaking sharply parallel to the radar, and then jogging back."

Wong straightened.

"How would the assault team get in if the SA-2 is there?" Skull asked.

He looked at Hawkins for the answer, but it was Wong who spoke, explaining that the helicopters would have two options—either the same corridor the Hogs took, or a slightly more direct route that took advantage of the terrain and anomalies in the SA-2's radar net. This path, which Wong preferred, would have the helicopters fly at roughly four feet above the ground for about five miles. While in theory the Hogs could do that as well, Wong's first route would allow them to use less fuel. It was also less stressful.

Not that a half hour's drive near serious antiaircraft radars and just out of reach of several flak guns wouldn't get the heart pumping.

"So what's at the base?" Skull asked.

"As of yesterday afternoon, just the six ZSU-23-4's, no missiles, no armor, and no discernible troops for that matter," said Wong. "This is the configuration, organized for attacks from the south and west, though the other directions could be covered as well. Beyond that, I have not had an opportunity to consult the latest information."

The ZSUs were mobile four-barreled antiaircraft artillery units. Ubiquitous and deadly, but the Hogs were used to dealing with them.

"When?" asked Skull.

"Dusk," said Hawkins. "We want to hit it just after seventeen hundred hours. We'll have a company's worth of men, no more, Apaches and you guys, and whatever other air support RAF can throw our way. We don't think there are a lot of people there," Hawkins added, shifting on his feet uneasily, as if he was trying to convince himself. "There are two buildings. My guys are rehearsing it right now with a squad of SAS men. They've taken buildings before."

Knowlington did a mental inventory of his squadron. He had four planes available; the question was which pilots to put in them. His best guys had spent an enormous amount of time in the air lately.

He could fill one of the seats himself.

No. Not anymore.

Why not? It wasn't like he was going to drink in the cockpit. That might be the one place he could trust himself.

"Bristol assured me that your people could be ready at short notice," said Paddington.

"With all due respect to Captain Wong, he's not in charge of getting the airplanes ready, or drawing up the duty roster, or even assessing the risks," said Skull. His fingers found the top of his temple, rubbing deep into the well behind the skull bone.

"Colonel, if you don't think you can do this, that's okay," said Hawkins.

"Don't worry, Captain. We're doing it," said Skull, getting up. "I just need to figure out who's had the most sleep."

7

Lieutenant William "BJ" Dixon stood on the concrete apron a few yards from the start of the runway, watching a bomb-laden Hog take off. It seemed like years since he'd seen such a sight, years since he'd sat in a cockpit himself.

It had only been a few days. But those days were each a separate lifetime.

Dixon had parachuted into Iraq with a covert Delta Force team looking for Scuds. On his second night in-country, he'd called in a strike on a probable nuclear-biological-chemical weapons bunker less than a hundred yards from his position. Then time blurred. He'd hauled a sergeant nearly twice his age and double his weight out from under the noses of a dozen Iraqi soldiers. He'd seen a woman gunned down in the Iraqi countryside for trying to warn him about a search party. His clothes were singed in the explosion of an Iraqi house whose sole occupant was a two-year-old child. He'd carried another Iraqi child, a boy perhaps six or seven, nearly to freedom, only to have the kid jump on a grenade meant for Dixon himself.

The boy's broken body floated before him in the hazy wake of the Hog engines as the green-hulled warplane waddled off the runway. Bits and pieces of flesh scattered in the wind, soot covering his chin.

Eyes open and clear, irises a brilliant green.

Why did God let that happen? Why the kid and not him? It was Dixon's job to die, not the boy's.

BJ rubbed his cheeks, then stared at his hands. He expected them to be black with soot, but they were clean.

There hadn't been time to bury the kid, or even do more than make sure he was dead. Dixon had been jerked away by the others on the team, strapped into a harness, and snatched from the ground by an MC-130E Combat Talon Fulton Surface-to-Air Recovery. Propelled through the air by a flying slingshot, he'd dangled in the wind before being cranked into the bay of the big combat cargo plane. The grenade, the kid, the plane blurred into the tunneling hush of air around his ears. Infinite shades of black and brown wove ribbons around his head as he rambled weightless, helpless, through space.

Had it happened at all?

He saw himself going to the child, bending down.

But he hadn't done that, had he? He'd stayed back, afraid of what he would see.

No, he'd been there, holding the kid when the grenade exploded. He remembered that specifically.

But no way he would have survived if he had held the kid.

But he remembered it, could feel the shock wave reverberating through his bones, shaking his arm nearly out of its socket.

Too much of this. He was losing his mind.

Dixon rubbed his fingers across his face and began walking toward Oz, Devil Squadron's maintenance area. Four of the squadron's eleven planes—they'd lost one earlier in the war—were being repaired and prepped for action. Techies swarmed back and forth, oblivious to him.

Dixon looked at his hands. His fingers ought to be filthy dirty, but they were clean, stark white, not even pink. The deep bruises on his ribs and arms had already begun to heal; soon, there'd be no trace of his ordeal.

Too much of this.

"Yo, BJ, what are you doing out of bed?"

Dixon turned. Captain John "Doberman" Glenon, one of the squadron's senior pilots, stood in front of an empty bomb trolley, shaking his head.

"What are you doing?" Doberman repeated. "You're supposed to be resting."

BJ shrugged.

"Restless?" Glenon didn't bother waiting for the obvious answer. "Come on. Colonel's rounding up some guys for a meeting. He'd probably want you there."

Without saying anything, Dixon fell in behind Doberman as he cut past the hangars and aircraft in a beeline for Hog Heaven, the squadron's headquarters building. Though several inches shorter than Dixon, Glenon threw his legs forward like he was flicking switchblades; Dixon fell steadily behind.

"Yo, Antman," Doberman shouted to a thin black lieutenant talking to a pair of women officers near the building.

Lieutenant Stephen Depray turned around abruptly.

"Come on. Old Man's looking for us," said Doberman.

"Excuse me, ladies," said Antman, bowing.

Ladies. Did anyone call women ladies anymore? Ladies—like it was all a fairy tale.

Maybe it was. Dixon's eyes seemed to have lost their focus, and stray sounds cluttered his ears. His boot kicked against the metal steps as he followed the others into the building. He caught his balance on the doorjamb, pushed inside. When the door slammed shut behind him, the muscles in his throat gripped at his windpipe and he felt claustrophobic.

Colonel Knowlington had commandeered Cineplex for the meeting. Cineplex, a largish open room with refrigerators, a microwave, and a couch, featured a massive big-screen TV, hence its name. The television had been turned off—Knowlington obviously meant business.

"Captain, Lieutenant," said the colonel as they entered. "BJ, what are you doing here?"

"I thought you wanted me, sir," said BJ.

Knowlington's eyes burned into his forehead.

Maybe that was where the soot was. Dixon reached his fingers to rub it away.

"All right, come on," said Skull. He looked past BJ. "Shotgun, Hack. Good. Close the door and let's get going."

Dixon sat in one of the metal folding chairs directly behind the couch, watching as Captain Wong whispered something to the colonel. Pink fluorescent light bathed the room, making it larger than Dixon remembered.

"Here's the deal," Knowlington told them, abruptly turning away from Wong. "We're still nailing down the details, but basically, the British have a few dozen commando teams working north of the border, just like Delta, looking for Scuds and doing some other work. They lost track of two men last night. They have reason to believe that the Iraqis grabbed them and that they're being held at an abandoned air strip in a city, or rather south of a city, up near the Euphrates. They're looking at a few other places as well. It's a long shot, but Delta is going in to check it out. They're taking RAF Chinooks, along with Apaches and us for cover. We hit right before nightfall."

"What's the lineup?" Doberman asked the colonel.

"Four planes, Maverick Gs, in case it gets dark and you need the infrared to see the targets. Load flares and cluster-bombs as well. Supposedly there's not much defense; guns, that's all. That may change, especially if the British are right about their guys being there. The idea is that it may just be a way station or holding spot until Baghdad figures out what to do with them." Knowlington glanced at Wong, who nodded. "Captain Wong should have the whole deal, or as much as there is, by 1400 hours, which is going to be very close to kickoff time. This isn't going to be a milk run."

"Good thing," said Shotgun. "I've been pretty bored lately."

The others laughed.

"I'm in," said Doberman.

"Me too," said Antman.

"I'll lead the flight."

Dixon bent his head to see the pilot who had said that. Standing near the couch, he had a large body for a fighter pilot and a head that seemed one size too large. It had to be Major Preston, who'd just replaced Major James "Mongoose" Johnson as the squadron DO. He'd been on the mission that towed Dixon home, but BJ hadn't been introduced yet, and in fact didn't even know Preston's first name.

"Good, Hack," Knowlington said. "I thought you'd want to take it."

"Hey, Colonel, you know we're all in," said Shotgun.

"You're not tired?" Knowlington asked.

"Tired? What the hell's that? I'm not sure I've heard that word."

"I think you've logged over two hundred hours since the air war began," said the colonel. His voice seemed cross.

"Shit, I didn't know we were supposed to keep track," said O'Rouke. "What's the record?"

Knowlington frowned, but then nodded.

"We scrapping tomorrow's mission?" Gunny asked. George "Gunny" McIntosh was a captain who had served as a liaison with a Marine unit in a special exchange program before joining Devil Squadron; his nickname had apparently been adapted from the term for a Marine master sergeant. He and Doberman were tasked for an early morning tank-plinking mission.

"Tomorrow's frag stands," said Skull. "Assuming you and Doberman can handle the turnaround."

"I can handle it," said Doberman.

"Good," said the commander. "There's an SA-2 site close to the base that you have to avoid. That's probably the most serious complication. There should be a Wild

Weasel in the area to handle it or anything else that comes up. Like I said, we're still working on the details."

"Film at eleven," said Shotgun.

"Antman, you're backup if somebody gets a cold," said Skull as the others laughed at Shotgun's joke.

"Yeah, okay."

Knowlington's frown deepened as he turned to look directly at Dixon. The lieutenant held the older man's stare.

He'd seen it all, the colonel: been to Vietnam, nailed at least three MiGs there, lost some wingmen, flown black missions against the Soviets in the '70s. The years had burned themselves into the flesh of his face, pulling the skin tight against the bones of his skull—probably not why he'd gotten his nickname, but appropriate now. He was wise and brave, the one guy you could always count on to tell you what to do, to come to you through the static and the bullshit.

But had he seen anything like a little boy convulsing with the shock of a grenade?

"There just isn't a slot for you on this ride, BJ," said the colonel. "I'm sorry."

"That's all right."

"I know you want back in the game. There'll be plenty of time."

Dixon shrugged, or thought he did. He didn't really care, one way or another.

He rubbed his chin with his hand and stared at his palm, whiter than the walls.

8

The temptation to jump in and lead the mission himself lingered even as he finished giving them the lowdown. Colonel Knowlington wanted nothing else in the world but to fly again, to grip his hand around the stick and push the plane's nose into a hail of antiaircraft fire.

And stay there until the plane caught fire? Did he have a death wish?

Better to go out that way than in disgrace.

Death wish—wasn't that what drinking *really* was?

Not for him.

He couldn't take the mission. He couldn't, in fact, stay on as commander any longer. He was finished.

Telling them would be impossibly hard. Cleaner to slip out, avoid the inevitable scene.

He'd do it tonight, after they were off. He'd make the calls as soon as this was taken care of, talk to the general, get the paperwork in order, slip over to Riyadh and then home. He had friends who could smooth the way.

Knowlington asked if there were any questions, scanning the pilots' faces one more time, indulging a twinge of nostalgia. He'd come to know them well:

Doberman, who walked through life with a chip on his shoulder because he was a good six or eight inches shorter than the rest of the world.

Dixon, the nugget who'd come to the Gulf with tons of raw skill but was as green as a fresh Christmas tree. Not green anymore, poor kid.

Hack, the former pointy-nose pilot who wanted Skull's job, and was now about to have it handed to him on a silver platter.

Gunny, whose two months with the Marines had convinced him he was a Marine. Antman, a Don Juan–type who seemed incapable of breaking a heart or saying a bad word about anyone.

And Shotgun—hell, what could you say about Shotgun? A first-class one-of-a-kind screwball who could fly with his eyes closed, nail his target, and then go back for more.

There were others in the room too, hundreds—ghosts he'd flown with, guys who'd saved his butts and whose butts he'd saved, a whole wing of them.

"Colonel, I'd like to see about that reconnaissance flight," prompted Wong from the sideline.

"Right. Let's get going." Skull snapped back to the present. "We'll brief the mission at 1400. Planes will be waiting."

He wasn't going. He was quitting.

"Hack, see me in my office a minute, would you?" he added, throwing himself toward the doorway and his duty. His tongue and throat felt as if they had been scraped by steel wool.

A quick drink would cure that.

Knowlington had flown with a thousand guys in all sorts of circumstances. Most of them had retired long ago.

How had they done it, what had they said?

Listen, the time's here, I'm getting on, got to watch out

*for my family, don't have the thrill, getting tired of the bull-
shit, need to make a little money for a bit. . . .*

"Colonel?"

Skull spun around in the hallway. Preston stopped short
and winced as if he expected Knowlington to slug him.

"What, Hack?"

"What's the deal?"

"I just told you. The British lost a pair of SAS commandos. There's a chance they're at that base. Not a very
good chance, but a chance."

"But—"

"That's the whole story."

For a brief moment, Skull felt like slugging him.

Knowlington and Preston had briefly worked together a
year before when they were both posted to the Pentagon—
Skull heading a working group on interservice Special Operations, Preston pulling temporary duty as snot-nosed
aide for a general who, among other things, hated Skull for
having helped kill one of his pet projects years before.
Preston had made noises about making an issue of Skull's
drinking—undoubtedly at the general's suggestion, though
Hack was enough of a prig to think about it on his own.
There had been rumors of disciplinary action, and a not-
too-subtle attempt to persuade Knowlington to retire. Skull
had had to go deep into the favor bank to derail the whole
mess.

And yet, he would freely and honestly admit that Hack
was a good pilot with a wide range of experience and a
good helping of natural ability. It was possible, even likely,
that Major Preston would make a decent commander.

God, Skull wanted a drink.

His anger dissipated. Without saying anything else,
Knowlington turned around and walked to his office.

"Colonel?"

Skull stopped at the door, his hand cold against the
metal knob.

"What, Major?"

"You want to see me, right? You just asked me to see
you."

"Let's just skip it, okay?" said Knowlington. And without waiting for an answer, he pushed inside, closing the door behind him.

9

Technical Sergeant Rebecca Rosen gave the radio aerial a gentle but firm tap, nudging the metal fin into its slot behind the cockpit. Draped on her stomach over the fuselage, she screwed it in quickly; the UHF/TACAN antenna had given her so much trouble going in, she feared it might just decide to jump off.

The metal fin atop the Hog wasn't much bigger than a CD case. Still, this was at least the third one she'd had to replace in the last four or five days. All had been pockmarked with bullets or shrapnel. Either the Iraqis were using special bullets that homed in on radio signals, or Devil Squadron pilots were putting their planes in places where they shouldn't be much too often.

Upside down even.

"Rosen, what the *hell* are you doing? Sleeping on the job?"

"No, Sergeant!" she shouted, bolting upright but not looking down at Sergeant Clyston.

"Another F-ing aerial?"

"Yes, Sergeant."

"Jeeze-us. These pilots are *not* taking care of my planes *properly.*"

"No, Sergeant, they're not. Damn sloppy of them," said Rosen, finishing with the aerial. She rolled off the plane and jumped down to the tarmac. "They have to be scraping the suckers when they're landing, because there is no way those ragheads could shoot them off. No way."

"Flying upside down, most likely."

"Don't know up from down, most of 'em."

Clyston grunted in agreement. "We ready to go?"

"Almost. Have to double-check the ECM pod." Rosen gestured toward the ALQ-119 on the wing.

"Older than me," said Clyston derisively of the ECM, which was the first dual-mode jammer ever put into operation.

"No way, Sergeant. But I bet you worked on it."

"Prob'ly," said the capo. He finally smiled.

A radical breakthrough when first developed, the ECM confused enemy radars by filling the air with noise as well as false signals. It had been around for a very long time, however, and was fairly useless against the more sophisticated weapons systems Iraq had, like the SA-6. Replacements had been promised, but some bean counter had decided that the A-10's didn't rate high enough to get them.

"We'll be ready," Rosen told her boss.

"I'm counting on it," said Clyston. He bunched his hands on his hips.

"You selling something, Sergeant?" Rosen asked.

Clyston made a show of glancing around, as if worried that another crew member was within earshot. In actual fact, no one who worked for the capo would be so foolish as to linger nearby without very good cause, and they would never, ever overhear something he didn't want them to. Ever.

Rosen sensed what Clyston was going to say, and felt her face warming even as he opened his mouth.

"Word has it you were asking after Lieutenant Dixon," said the chief master sergeant in his most tactful tone.

"I was inquiring about his health, yes," she said, trying to make her voice as flat as possible. Anyone else she would have told to screw off, but there was no way in the world to say that to the capo. No way.

Clyston's large chest heaved upward in an exaggerated sigh. He shook his head, but said nothing. Rosen found her bottom lip starting to tremble; she tried biting at it, but her teeth couldn't quite clamp down.

Anybody else would have gotten a double barrel of invective, maybe even a good swing. Anybody else, she probably wouldn't have cared.

But Sergeant Clyston was—well, Sergeant Clyston.

"Sergeant, is my work unacceptable?" she asked, doing her best to keep her lip from shaking.

"That's not what this is about, Sergeant."

"Sergeant." She clamped her mouth shut, unable to say anything else. She steadied her eyes, hoping they wouldn't water.

Damn, damn, damn. This shit had never happened to her before.

Rosen put her head down, waiting for the inevitable lecture. Clyston was right, of course; enlisted and officers didn't mix. She and Dixon had nothing in common—she was older than him, for christsakes.

But damn, damn, damn.

"Sergeant, these planes have to be ready to fly at 1400 sharp," snapped Clyston. "Then I'd appreciate it if you helped Vincenzi on that F-in' engine. He's having a hell of a time."

"Yes, Sergeant," she said, though Hog engines were hardly her specialty. "Be glad to."

"I appreciate it. Vinchy makes a hell of a sauce, but he doesn't always boil the spaghetti right, if you know what I mean."

"Yes, Sergeant."

Rosen listened until the scrape of his boots told her he was far away before wiping her wet cheek with her sleeve.

10

Captain Kevin Hawkins wrapped his hand around the tubular frame of his seat as the British Chinook abruptly jerked itself off the runway, its Lycoming engines whipping the twin rotors in a fury. His SAW—an M249 light machine gun or Squad Automatic Weapon, also known as an FN Minimi—slipped against his leg as the big helicopter bucked forward. He jerked his hand to grab the rifle, and nearly spilled his cup of tea.

"I thought you said your aircraft were smooth," he said to the sergeant next to him on the canvas bench.

SAS Sergeant Millard Burns turned slowly toward Hawkins and nodded in his methodical way, a bob down, a bob up. At fifty feet above ground level the helicopter abruptly stopped climbing, leaving her rear end angled slightly as she sped northwards, finally steady enough for Hawkins to sip his drink.

The nose of the team's other helicopter, carrying most of the British commandos, appeared in the window above the opposite bench. The Chinook—or "heli" as the British soldiers tended to refer to the craft—had a splotchy camouflage that blended dark green with pink splashes of paint. Referred to as "desert pink" by the Royal Air Force crew, it was the oddest scheme Hawkins had ever seen.

"Good chaps?" said Burns, nodding at the six Delta troopers parked along the benches toward the front of the aircraft. Besides Burns, there were three more British paratroopers aboard this Chinook—Splash One—and a dozen SAS men and their captain aboard the second, Splash Two.

"The best," Hawkins said. All of the D boys had been with him on missions north of the border before. He'd known three—Jerry Fernandez, Kevin Smith, and Peter Crowley—for nearly five years. Armand Krushev and Stephen "Pig" Hoffman had won medals for their still-classified exploits in Panama right before the invasion. And Juan Mandaro was a five-tools player; a communications and sniper expert with a (civilian) EMT badge and a knack for blowing things up, Mandaro had particularly sharp vision and rated among the best point men Hawkins had ever seen in combat.

"Your guys?" Hawkins asked the British sergeant, taking a stab at conversation only because Burns seemed to need to talk.

"Top. Been in hot water before. Squaddies began in Ireland together. Tight after that."

Hawkins had not-so-distant relatives in Belfast, children and grandchildren of the grandmother who had first turned him on to tea. At least one belonged to the IRA Provos—the SAS's enemy in Ireland. He grunted noncommittally, turning his attention back to his cup.

"Jundies won't know what hit them when we go in," added Burns.

"Jundies?"

"Ragheads. The Iraqis."

"Oh, yeah."

Burns reached into the pocket of his uniform and took out the map of their target. They'd gone over the plan at least twenty times before taking off, mapping contingen-

cies and psyching out possible Iraqi moves; there was no
practical benefit to reviewing it now. But maps, even
roughly sketched ones, held almost supernatural power for
some guys, and apparently the British NCO was one of
them. The trace of his finger across the shallow berm near
the road, the double tap of his thumb against the blocks
representing buildings—these were part of a holy ritual
that he undoubtedly believed would guarantee success.

Some men preferred to continually check their
weapons, making sure ammo belts weren't kinked, triple-
checking the taped trigger spoons on the grenades, testing
the sharpness of their battle knives. Hawkins liked to drink
his tea.

"We'll have the carriageway right off," said Burns.

He meant the road. Two Apaches would cut off access
to the base. Once the Hogs took the Zeus guns out, the plan
would be boom-boom, teams at each building, top and bottom. Three stories. Neither had defenses, and it looked
from the surveillance "snaps," as the British put it, that one
was completely unoccupied.

You never could tell.

Hawkins leaned his head back against the wall of the
helicopter, trying to ignore the vibration as well as the
sergeant without success on either front.

"Moons and Puff will move with your men to the second house," said Burns, repeating a sentence he'd repeated
now at least three times since they'd met. "I'll be with you
on the first."

Hawkins's attention drifted. An RAF reconnaissance
Tornado would zoom over the small base roughly ten minutes before the Chinooks were to land. It would check the
defenses one last time. The A-10's would pound anything
that had materialized and then clear the assault teams and
the supporting Apaches in.

Standard house-clearing tactics—flash-bang grenades,
shotguns, MP-5's, in and out.

Very fast. Probably nothing there, but if not, why the
flak guns?

Though they came from different armies, the troopers

and the commandos were equipped roughly the same. The SAS men carried American M-16 Armalites with grenade launchers, just as some of the D boys did; they all tended to refer to the guns as 203's after the M203 designation for the launcher. They also had two Minimis on their team. Three of Hawkins's men carried silenced MP5's, very light and nasty submachine guns that the commandos were also familiar with; two others had Mossberg shotguns. Altogether, the commandos and troopers carried a large number of grenades, the nastiest of which was arguably the white phosphorus, or phos to the SAS men; the ingredients could burn through unprotected skin and eat a man's body. Among their other tasty treats were 66mm man-launched antiarmor rockets, modern-day disposable bazookas that could take out most modern tanks.

"Hit at last light," said Burns.

"Yeah," said Hawkins, barely paying attention.

"I've heard your A-10's are slower than fuckin' helicopters," said the sergeant. "Will they be of use?"

"I wouldn't worry about the Hogs," Hawkins told him.

"You've worked with the A-10's before?" asked Burns.

"Oh, yeah," said Hawkins. "Mean bastards."

"Fuckin' ugly."

"Yeah," said the captain.

"Ugly's good."

"The best," said Hawkins.

11

Hack's heart picked up its beat as he neared the border with Iraq. The contrails of a flight of bombers arced across the top quarter of his windscreen; black clouds of smoke lined the horizon to his right. To his left, faint flickers of light—maybe reflections, maybe tracers—glinted in the dust of the desert floor.

It was one thing to haul ass across the border at thirty thousand feet in the world's most advanced fighter jet, when the flex of your muscle could increase your thrust exponentially and take you to Mach 2. It was quite another to be coaxing a Maverick-laden Hog through fifteen thousand feet, hoping for a tailwind to boost you to three hundred knots.

Why had he taken this damn A-10 assignment?

Because he had no choice. Because it would get him where he wanted to go—squadron commander, colonel, general. Beyond.

Why the hell had he volunteered for this mission?

Knowlington had put him up to it. The colonel knew damn well that if he didn't volunteer, he'd look like a chickenshit to the rest of the squadron.

Stinking Knowlington, so full of himself, so cocksure that he was still the hottest stick on the patch. If he was so hot, why the hell hadn't he taken the mission himself?

He would have, if Hack hadn't raised his hand. Show him up.

Maybe not.

One thing Hack had to say for Knowlington—the SOB didn't seem to be drinking, or at least he was a hell of a lot more careful about it here than in Washington.

He would sooner or later, though. Then Hack would take over the squadron, move on with the game plan. Get his own squadron, make his mark, transfer back into a real plane. A lot of older guys were choking the path to promotion, but he could cut around them with a good job here.

Which was why he'd volunteered for the gig. Kick some butt in a major mission. Somebody would be bound to notice.

It was more than that. Hack was ambitious, no denying that. Nor could he deny—to himself—that he felt he'd screwed up on this morning's mission and wanted to redeem himself.

Not screwed up. Just gotten scared when he didn't have to be scared.

But he'd volunteered for the Splash package simply because he felt like he ought to be in the mix. He belonged on the toughest assignments. Prestige, ego, redemption, and all that other bullshit were beside the fact.

Preston tried to push the fatigue away, focusing his eyes on the navigation gear, checking his way-points, mentally projecting himself against the sketched lines of his flight plan.

"Two minutes to border," he told his flight.

The others acknowledged. Once more, he had O'Rourke as his wingman. Doberman in Devil Three had Gunny on his six. The Hogs would work in pairs above the target, with Preston and Shotgun on the east side on the first run, Glenon and his wingman the west.

Preston nudged his stick as he came over the border, then gave his instruments a quick check. His fuel burn seemed a tiny bit high; it was barely noticeable, but it might be a problem later on, stealing valuable minutes over the target area. He told himself to try to make up for it if he could.

Checks complete, he rocked his body back and forth in the ejection seat, coaxing away the knots and aches. In some ways, this was the worst part of any mission—the long middle. You could easily be lulled to inattention. Worse, a tired pilot might fall asleep.

Like nearly every other pilot in the service, Hack had a stash of pep pills in his flight suit for emergency use. But he hated the idea of using them, and in fact had taken an amphetamine only once in his life, and that was in college cramming for a test. He didn't even like aspirin or antibiotics. He'd accepted his anthrax shot before coming to the Gulf only because he figured he would be court-martialed if he refused.

He hit his way-marker, nudging ten more degrees east as they prepared to leg around the SA-2 coverage area south of Splash.

The missile complex had been hit earlier in the war. Hack suspected that its gear had been so damaged by early Allied raids that all it could manage was a baneful bleep, the rattle of an empty scabbard. But there'd be no way to tell until it launched a few flying telephone poles.

If it did that, a Weasel would nail it. A Phantom was flying patrol circuits in the area, ready for the SA-2 and anything else that might pose a threat.

Hack checked his watch—they were right on schedule.

In exactly 120 seconds, an RAF Tornado would fall out of the sky near the river ahead and blaze over the abandoned Iraqi base. The Tornado's high-tech cameras would take one last look at the base before the ground teams went in. If they spotted any antiaircraft guns or SAMs, the Hogs would hit them just before the RAF Chinooks came in range.

"Devil Flight, this is Splash One," said a voice with a British upper-crust accent as they hit the next-to-last way-marker before arriving at the target. "Position, please."

As Hack clicked to acknowledge the transmission from the helicopter, the RWR went off—an Iraqi ground-intercept radar had just come up ahead.

Several voices clogged the circuit. Somewhere in the middle of the static, Hack hoped, was the voice of the F-4 Wild Weasel pilot.

Hack waited for the cacophony to clear, then calmly acknowledged Splash One, giving his position and asking how far the helos were from setting down.

Before the Splash pilot could respond, an AWACS controller further south barked out a warning: Break ninety. A short-ranged but potent Roland missile battery north of the target area had turned itself on.

The controller called for the Hogs to make a hard turn, taking them out of harm's way. But because of the proximity of the SA-2 site and defenses to the east, it would mean the Hogs would have to backtrack around to pick up the proper vector into the target. That would screw up their timing and eat into their fuel reserves.

Weasel would nail the Roland, which couldn't hit them from where it was anyway. Screw 'em.

"Break ninety," repeated the AWACS.

"Negative," said Hack quickly. "Devil Flight stay on course. Acknowledge."

"Two. Kick butt," said Shotgun.

"Three. We're right behind you."

Before Gunny could respond from Devil Four, the AWACS crewman blurted out a fresh and ominous warning—the Iraqis had launched two missiles.

12

RAF Captain John Conrad started to laugh as the Panavian Tornado hurtled toward the ground. The Turbo-Union RB1999 Mk104 engines were in fine mettle. The nose of the plane shuddered slightly, then smoothed out, the jet's speed sliding over Mach 1.2. The altimeter ladder nudged downward, breaking through three thousand feet as the world rushed brown and black, an abstract splatter of paint and speed dashing at odd angles around him. Conrad laughed and laughed, riding the adrenaline of the high-speed run. Wings tucked tight at a sixty-seven-degree sweep, the plane shot smooth toward the ragged terrain, knifing through the low-level turbulence. Conrad pulled back on the stick, leveling off just under a thousand feet, spotting the long gray splotch of his target area ahead.

The pilot giggled to himself as he held the plane steady so his backseat systems operator or "nav" could manage the sophisticated array of reconnaissance equipment in the weapons bay. Three BAe infrared cameras and a Vinten

Linescan 4000 IR surveillance system filled the hold originally designed for a 27mm IWKA-Mauser cannon. Together, the wide-angle line-scan and thermal-image modules probed every inch of the Iranian base. Conrad counted off three seconds, saw two matchboxes at the edge of the rectangle, and then he was beyond them; he yanked back on his stick, climbing quickly, gravity smacking him in the chest. He pushed the Tornado to the left as blue sky filled the canopy, the altimeter ladder galloping upward, mission accomplished.

"Good go, Sister Sadie. Oh, good go, my girl," he told his plane. The recon ship had been named partly for a Beatles song, and partly for the buxom tart bending over her nose. Conrad's squadron included one of the best nose-art painters in the RAF.

The pilot asked his backseater if he had enough data.

"Not quite sure," said the navigator, Lieutenant Charles Nevins. Besides the normal Tornado backseater duties, as recon officer Nevins handled an array of sensors that included an infrared camera. "Revetment empty. Zeus 23's on the hill and below the field."

"Missiles?"

"Didn't seem so."

"Need another run?" asked the pilot, barely containing his enthusiasm.

"SA-6 eight miles north of Splash. They're tracking," warned the nav.

"Let's have a go. Yank Weasel will take care of the missiles," said Conrad, and before his lieutenant could answer he had knifed the Tornado back toward the Iraqi runway.

Originally designed as a long-range interceptor, the Panavian Tornado lacked the furball maneuverability of frontline American fighters. It could, however, go very, very fast, and its terrain-following radar and quick-response engines allowed it to do so in all sorts of situations, day and night. In fact, to Captain Conrad, this mission was rather bland—clear sailing in daylight without nearby defenses to worry about.

But it was still a hell of lot of fun. Flying was always a lot of fun.

"SAM tracking," shouted his nav, warning that there was another antiair battery hunting them. "ECMs!"

"Stay on it," Conrad said, winding the Tornado's altimeter toward zero.

As the rectangular shape of the abandoned runway came into view, Conrad cut hard left to run over it, speed washing from the plane. He was at five hundred feet, three hundred, still lower, getting personal with his target. He pushed his wings level, saw a speckle of something out ahead of him, then felt a light thump as he pulled the plane upward. The smell of fried chicken filled the cockpit—the Tornado had mashed through a flock of birds, sizzling at least one of them.

"Clean!" yelled the navigator. Either the ECMs or their hard maneuvers or both had shaken the Iraqi defenses. The radar warning screen, which had shown the missile battery's radar to be quite some distance to the west, was now blank.

Conrad banked south, quickly reorienting himself. The A-10A's escorting the Chinooks blipped on the radar screen, just over fifty miles away. The helicopters should be somewhere nearby, but Conrad was no longer interested in them—his job now was to get home. He sailed through his turn, running to the west. The Tornado's altimeter nudged through six thousand feet and headed toward ten. He was north of the Euphrates, circling south in the same area as the base, lining up for his getaway leg home.

"More guns beyond the runway," announced the navigator. "Nothing big."

"Tank?"

"No."

"Other defenses?"

"Road south of the base, bunker, maybe just a defensive post." The navigator's voice trailed off as he checked the videotaped sensor image. "Maybe some cached weapons there. Can't tell."

"Jolly good. Feed the Yanks the positions of the guns,

and remind them where the SA-6 was in case the Weasel hasn't gotten her yet."

"Right."

But before the backseater could hail Devil Flight, their detection gear threw up another radar warning.

"Roland on us. Where'd that come from? Fuckers, fuckers!" The navigator's voice hit an octave so high Conrad thought his helmet's faceplate would break.

"ECMs," Conrad said calmly, though of course the instruction was unnecessary; his backseater was already trying to jam the enemy trackers. The Roland—a German missile—was a nasty medium-range missile that could detect an aircraft at roughly ten miles and nail it around four. The RWR had it pegged straight ahead, five miles away, two miles northwest of Splash.

"Missiles in the air! Missiles!" yelped the nav.

Once launched, the Roland moved at roughly 1.5 times the speed of sound, somewhat slower than the Tornado was capable of. But Conrad was in a poor position to outrun it; his best bets were the countermeasures his beackseater was furiously working, along with the fact that the Roland had been launched from just beyond its lethal envelope.

Not that he intended on standing still. He flooded the afterburners and pushed the Tornado into a sharp jink. Newton's Laws struck him with a vengeance, gravity smashing every inch of his body. He flicked his wrist left, flicked right; the fly-by-wire controls faithfully fought the turbulent shock waves to fulfill his commands, whipping the plane back and forth to accentuate the confusion.

"Lost one!" yelped the navigator, but the words barely registered. Conrad could feel the second missile, gunning for him. It had somehow managed to follow his twists and was now behind him, burning through its second stage in an all-out effort to bring him down.

But if it was a race, Conrad was going to win. He shut out the voices blaring in his headphones, shut out the blur of the sky, the rumble of the jets, the hard rush of gravity against his chest and face. His fingers were wrapped on the throttle, holding the Turbo-Unions at the firewall.

It came down to him and the missile and the plane. Sister Sadie wasn't giving in and neither was he.

Roland would be reaching the end of its range now.

A fresh rush of adrenaline hit Conrad's veins. He was going to make it; he had it.

This sure as fuck was fun.

"Come on, you bleedin' bugger," he yelled at the missile, laughing again. "Hit me, fucker. I dare you. I dare you."

And then it did.

13

Hack steadied his hand on the stick. At least three different transmissions overran each other on the radio. His RWR blared, and he could see a furious geyser of antiaircraft artillery rising in the sky off his right wing.

He had the missiles beamed, riding away from their Doppler radar in a way that made his airplane invisible to their seeker. In any event, they didn't seem to be looking for him.

It wasn't clear from the cacophony in his headset whether the Weasel had launched at the battery or not. Nor was he sure where the Tornado was.

The SAM launcher seemed to be about eight miles to the northwest of his position, which would put it about two, maybe three from the target—damn close when they attacked, well within its lethal range.

Depending on how well the Iraqis were trained, it could take them a while to reload the double-launcher.

Or not.

Hack looked for the Tornado. It had swept north after its second recon run, and should be coming back at him, overhead and to the left.

An English voice broke through the radio static, but Hack couldn't decipher the words as another excited voice filled the frequency, an F-16 pilot screaming that he was being targeted in another encounter far from here. The voice burst loud, then cleared, as if it were a figment of his imagination.

"Splash One is zero-eight from Splashdown," said the pilot of the lead helicopter, apparently unaware of what was going on. "Sister Sadie, what's our sitrep?"

As if in answer, a large gray cloud blossomed in the northwest sky. An orange dot pricked through the gray, then disappeared.

"I'm hit," said the RAF pilot a few seconds later. "Wing damage."

"Splash One and Two, hold your positions," Hack told the helicopters. He then asked for radio silence. "Everyone, hold your transmissions. Sister Sadie, give your position."

Preston heard only the hard pull of his own breath. He glanced at his warning radar—clean. Nudging his stick gently to the left, he rode the Hog in the direction of the Tornado.

And the Rolands.

"Sister Sadie, repeat," he said.

A garbled tangle of words answered him; Hack deciphered "hit," but nothing else.

"I can see him," said Doberman in Devil Three. He gave a heading and then his own position—Glenon was at least three miles further north than he should have been.

"Watch yourself," answered Hack.

"I'm on you," said Doberman, obviously in contact with the RAF plane though Hack couldn't pick up the British pilot's response.

"You're hit bad. Bail," said Doberman finally.

Hack tried hailing Sister Sadie on the Emergency Guard frequency, but got no response.

"Missile away," said a distant voice.

The Weasel, launching on the site.

"What are we doing?" asked Shotgun. The last part of his transmission was overrun by the F-16 flight again.

"I need radio silence here," barked Hack. "Devil Three, stay with him. Two, you're on my back."

Preston slid southward, trying to psych out where exactly the Tornado pilot would go out. The assault team was behind him and on his left; the Tornado, Doberman, and his wingman ought to be crossing straight ahead.

"What's going on?" asked Splash One.

"Hold your position," Hack told him. "Repeat, all Splash aircraft, hold your position."

And shut the hell up, he wanted to add.

A brown and red stone shot into his windscreen, a meteor tossed down from space. Hack jerked his head back, taken by surprise before realizing it was the Tornado, several miles off, flames spitting from one of the wings.

He'd never seen a plane on fire before. It didn't seem to be a plane at all. It didn't seem real.

Doberman and his wingman were lower, much lower, tracking southward behind the stricken plane.

What the hell had Doberman been doing so far north?

"Bail out, Sister Sadie! Bail out!" Hack said, pushing the mike button.

"Rolands are still hot! They're gunning for you, Doberman!" said Shotgun over the squadron frequency.

"Fuck them," said Doberman.

Hack's RWR lit up, warning of a fresh salvo of antiaircraft missiles. Where the hell was that Weasel and his SAM killers?

14

Doberman cursed as a wave of turbulence buffeted his wings, shaking the Hog so hard his head nearly hit the canopy despite his snugged restraints.

The Iraqis had launched two more missiles, maybe at the Tornado and maybe at him.

"Chaff and go lower," he told Gunny in Devil Four, hoping his wingman had the good sense to take evasive maneuvers and not hang on him as he continued to track the stricken RAF plane. "Sister Sadie, if you're getting out, now's the time to go."

The British pilot said something in return, but static swallowed his words. The rear quarter of the plane was engulfed in flames, and yet it flew on seemingly untroubled by the massive damage, picking up speed as it flashed over Doberman.

"Don't you have ejection seats in those fucking planes?" Doberman shouted.

The red flames were replaced by a large, hairy spider

that grew in an instant and disappeared. Doberman cursed, then yanked his plane hard to the left, pushing out electronic tinsel in case the Rolands were still behind him.

Which they were.

The Roland was designed as a medium-range surface-to-air missile system, intended to work as part of a more comprehensive antiair net, but nasty enough on its own. One of the things that made it particularly difficult to defeat was its ability to track very-low-flying objects; once the missile attached itself to your back, it could trail you even if you dove below fifty feet.

Glenon knew that, but hitting the deck was his only defense—the missile was several times faster than the Hog, hard to fool with tinsel, and couldn't be defeated by the primitive ECM pod slung beneath the A-10's wing. Doberman and his wingman had only one thing going for them: They were flying Hogs. They slashed across the terrain, throwing out electronic tinsel as they cut, hoping the missiles would grab for the electronic ghosts, or at least hesitate enough for the Hogs to get away.

Doberman pushed his nose into the dirt, braving the buffeting wind as he ran less than thirty feet from the desert floor. And he urged the missiles onto his back—no way could he live with himself if they took out Gunny.

The warning gear snapped clear. Either he'd ducked the missiles or they were about to crunch his tail fins.

Doberman pulled back on the stick, taking a half breath as he twisted his head, searching for his wingman. A tree of smoke filled the left quarter of his canopy—one of the Rolands had exploded on the ground. Glenon jerked his attention to the other side, and spotted a dark green hulk running off his right wing, almost behind him, flying so low he thought for a second it was a truck.

"You okay, Four?"

"They tell me I am," said Gunny. "Six is clean. Rolands went off course and splashed in the grass. Weasel says he got 'em, but I want pictures."

"You're starting to sound like Shotgun."

"Aw, shucks. I'm blushing."

"Three." Doberman pushed the Hog's nose up, trying to puzzle out where he was.

"Devil Three, acknowledge," said Preston, his voice blurring into static as the rest of his transmission was lost.

"Three. Didn't hear a word you said, Hack."

"Are you okay?"

"We're fine." Doberman snapped his finger off the transmit button. What did the fuckhead think? Just because he wasn't flying a fast-mover he couldn't duck SAMs?

"Weasel reports Rolands are down. SA-2 is not active. Watch the guns at Splashdown. What's your position?"

Gunny's excited voice broke in before Doberman could answer.

"Two chutes! Two chutes! I have two parachutes off my nose, two miles maybe. Shit! Those bastards are luckier than a dog in a whorehouse!"

15

Captain Conrad watched as his backseater hit the ground a good twenty seconds ahead of him, tucking his feet and falling over into the sand. The wind took the nav's parachute, pitching him along the ground like a bag tossed into a hurricane.

That was all the hint Conrad needed—he got his legs moving as he touched down and worked the snaps off with his hands, hoping to release the chute and step off like a pro. He undid one snap but not the other, and ended up dragged along as ignobly as his backseater. The wind was so strong it finally yanked the chute away, freeing his shoulder but sending him into a wild spin in the dirt. Conrad rolled several yards before his momentum finally gave out.

When he realized he had stopped, he did a push-up to his knees, then began laughing uncontrollably.

Damn sight for anyone to see, he thought; good thing

his squadron mates hadn't been along or he'd never hear the end of it.

As Conrad hauled off his helmet, the ground shook with the roar of an approaching jet. A pair of American A-10's whipped directly overhead, no more than thirty feet off the desert sand—so close, in fact, that he thought for a moment the Yanks might reach out a hand and try to grab him.

They didn't. But they circled back so low and slow, he could see the lead pilot give him a thumbs-up. He waved, then ran to Charlie.

"Up and at 'em, Charles," he told the lieutenant, who was hunched over the sand.

"Stomach's not right," said the backseater, leaning to retch.

Not terribly anxious to succumb to the power of suggestion, Conrad quickly backed away. He took out his emergency radio, dialing in the distress frequency. The A-10A pilot answered his hail in under thirty seconds.

"Bravo Baker," he said, beginning the elaborate recognition procedure, which would culminate with a series of personal questions about his mum to prove he was who he said he was.

"Fuck that," answered the Yank. "I'm Doberman. You guys okay?"

"Tip-top," said Conrad.

"Yeah. Hang tight while we figure this out."

"Quite."

"Come again?"

"Ten-four," Conrad told him, trying to toss up a little American slang.

"What the fuck are you saying?"

"Standing by," he responded. The wind howled, shoving gritty sand into his eyes; Conrad removed his gloves to clear them, then retrieved his sunglasses from his suit for protection. By now the sun had set, and the dark glasses turned the landscape into a mass of shadows, blurry grays and blacks like walls being moved toward him. Conrad lifted the glasses slightly away from his face, holding them like shields against the dust and looking sideways. A thick cyclone of soot rose directly south of him—Sister Sadie.

He trotted over to his navigator, who was now sitting cross-legged on the desert sand. Nevins had pulled off his survival vest and found a cap and scarf in his gear.

"You look like a nomad," Conrad joked.

"Fucking wind," said Nevins, reaching into a flap pocket on his pant leg. He removed a pair of goggles.

"Thanks," said Conrad, grabbing them.

"Fuck!"

"Make sure your radio works," Conrad told him. "Quickly. Our contact is Devil Three—Doberman. Go on."

Nevins took out the radio reluctantly, still a little jittery with stomach upset as he hooked in the earplug. As soon as Conrad saw that Nevins had hailed the Yank, he began trotting away.

"Hey! Hey!" shouted the nav.

"I'll be back!" Conrad told him, turning and running backward. "Have to pay my respects." He wheeled and ran for all he was worth toward the wreckage of their plane, more than a mile away.

16

Hawkins had trouble both hearing the copilot and keeping his balance as the Chinooks hovered above a stretch of empty desert about twenty-five miles southwest of their target. Worse, he couldn't figure out what the hell was going on. He knew the reconnaissance Tornado had gone down—but what about the target? Was it clean, hot, or what?

"Devil One isn't answering," said the copilot.

"Try again."

"Sergeant Williams in Splash Two wants you." Tired of trying to act as a go-between, the copilot slipped the bulky British headset back to Hawkins, who held it to his ear, bracing himself against the back of the seat with his leg.

"What's up?" he asked the SAS sergeant who was heading the commando team in Splash Two.

"My question to you," answered the sergeant.

"I'm trying to figure it out. We don't have target data."

"Heli pilot's worried about sand getting in his engines," said the sergeant.

"So's ours," Hawkins told him.

"Losing light."

Hawkins and his men were used to working at night, but neither the Apaches nor the Hogs were equipped with the sophisticated gear that would allow them to support a night operation. Nor were the Chinooks or the SAS teams fully equipped to do so. Escaping as night fell was one thing, but run into serious defenses and the darkness could work against them.

Defenses that could take down a Tornado were by definition serious. But was the missile at the site, or was it one of the launchers several miles away that they'd been briefed about? If it was the latter, moving ahead was an acceptable risk.

But they had to go *now*.

"Stand by, Splash Two," Hawkins told the British sergeant. He tapped the copilot, who'd turned his attention to his instruments. "Can you get me Devil One?"

"I'll try. Wind is kicking up fierce down here," he added. "One of your Apaches is turning back."

"What?"

"Engine trouble. The sand, no doubt."

"Get me the fucking Hogs. Right now. Shit."

17

Everything was falling apart. They had a plane down deep in enemy territory. They had no intelligence on the landing zone, and had lost the element of surprise.

And now one of the Apaches had engine trouble.

None of it was Hack's fault, and yet there was a hole in the side of his stomach. He tried to fight off the doubt that crept all around him, tried to focus on the rapidly dimming landscape outside his canopy. It wasn't too late; they could still nail this thing down if he kept his head, if everyone kept their heads.

"Devil One, Devil One," squawked one of the British helicopter pilots, though he didn't identify himself. "What is this situation? We need a sitrep. Repeat, sitrep."

"Devil One. British craft, identify yourself."

Static.

As he transmitted again, Preston checked his fuel to see how much he'd lost trying to track down the Tornado and stay clear of the missiles.

A hunk. At best he had forty minutes of linger time left. The assault team was supposed to be on the ground for a good hour.

A new voice came back from the RAF Chinook— Hawkins.

"Devil One, this is Splash Commander. Can you give me the situation?"

"Sister Sadie is down; we're attempting to establish contact," he told Hawkins.

"What's the sit at Splashdown?"

"I'm still working on that," said Preston. "Sadie was hit before he could tell us."

"We need to know *now*."

"No shit, Captain," Hack said. He hated the Delta ass-hole—he was tempted, sorely tempted, to tell him to just go ahead and fly north—right into the frickin' SAMs.

"Repeat?" asked Hawkins.

Hack hated everyone and everything connected with this stinking operation, the RAF crew for getting shot down, Knowlington for making him take the mission.

He hated himself. He was blowing it big-time.

How close was that Roland? Was it still live, or had the Weasel smashed it?

"Hold for now. I'll get to you when I know something," he told Hawkins, abruptly flipping back to the squadron frequency and hailing Doberman.

"Are you in contact with Sadie?"

"Affirmative."

"Nice of you to tell me."

"I've been trying to raise you," said Doberman.

"Does Coyote know?" he asked, referring to the AWACS control plane, which would alert SAR assets and coordinate a rescue.

"Can't raise him either," said Doberman.

The whole damn mission was going to hell.

"Hold on. I'll take care of it," said Preston, who needed to talk to the AWACS about the Roland anyway.

"Shit, we have company," said Doberman.

"Repeat, Three."

"Vehicles, three vehicles. Must be homing in on our boy's transmission. Shit."

"Smoke 'em," cut in Shotgun.

"Yeah, no shit," responded Doberman. "Gunny, on my back."

"Covered."

Preston went back to Hawkins. "Splash One. Give me your position."

"We're in the same fucking position we were in ten minutes ago. What is the situation at Splashdown? Repeat. What is the situation—"

Hack pushed the transmit button before Hawkins finished. The mission was dead now. There was no sense sending the assault team to rescue men who might or might not be there, when there were two downed fliers who needed help ASAP.

"Splash One, stand by for coordinates to pick up Sister Sadie's crew."

"Fuck you," sputtered Hawkins.

"Fuck yourself," said Hack. "Stand by for coordinates. Iraqi vehicles en route. We're on them."

He could see Doberman starting to dive to the north, and worked out a vector and distance for the Chinook.

"Tell the helicopter pilot to look for the burning trucks ten miles to your north," he added. "Go!"

18

In life, Tornado GR.Mk 1A ZA981 SS Sister Sadie had worn a speckled brown coat, the latest fashion in desert dress. In death, she wore a very appropriate black, her twisted frame wrenched across about a quarter of a mile of shadowy desert. Her arms had been shorn off and her tail scattered into several bits, but Conrad was interested specifically in her fuselage—and even more specifically in the mission tapes, which would show what her sensors had recorded.

Always an agreeable girl, Sadie had had the good sense to wedge herself into the dirt at only a slight angle, making it comparatively easy for the pilot to pick his way through the mangled metal and retrieve the video.

Except that the cartridge refused to budge.

"Haven't all day, Sadie," Conrad complained, but the stricken plane refused to give up her prize. The pilot stepped back, unholstered his personal pistol—a German Glock, as it happened, not quite official RAF issue—and fired a salvo at the locking mechanism guarding the access panel.

Sadie groaned, but the foreign bullet glanced harmlessly away.

Conrad tried again. This time, the ricochet nearly skinned the side of his face.

He threw himself against the plane, this time putting the gun to much better use as a hammer. Smashing back and forth, he was finally able to wedge the barrel in and use it as a lever. He paused, took out the gun, and was contemplating a fresh attack—when the tape inexplicably spat out.

"Thanks, Sadie."

Conrad slapped the plane on her fuselage, then stood back and gave her a proper salute. But any temptation to linger was overwhelmed by the sound of trucks approaching across the desert. He took two steps away, turning to his right as the vehicles emerged from the shadows, ripping through the dust no more than a quarter mile away. They must be coming for the wreckage, he thought, starting to run, but as he did a grenade or a light howitzer shell landed less than fifty yards away, throwing him forward in the grit.

That was just as well—a machine gun began firing from one of the vehicles, its stream of red tracers slicing through the air only a few inches from his head.

And then a roar from above overwhelmed the noise of the Iraqi vehicles and their hellish gunfire. The rattling sound could only properly be described as the snort from a very angry animal.

A Hog, as a matter of fact.

Conrad's guardian angels had arrived.

19

Doberman nudged his rudder pedals, lining up the crosshairs on the shadow closest to the downed Tornado. Before he could press the trigger, red sparks spewed from his target.

"Aim higher," he told the enemy armored personnel carrier. Then his thumb danced over the control stick, first to one side, then the other. "Bing-bang-boing," he said, unleashing a flood of spent uranium at the Iraqi vehicle. The spray decimated the nasty Iraqi, hot water eliminating a spider. Doberman worked his pedals, pushing his aim toward a second shadow; another bing-bang-boing and over a hundred shells erased the second Iraqi vehicle, this one a pickup truck with some type of medium-sized gun mounted over the cab.

Glenon pulled back, sweeping around as he temporarily lost his bearings in the dark shadows of the fast-approaching night.

"I have someone moving near the plane," said Gunny,

viewing the scene through his Maverick's IR seeker in Devil Four.

"Pilot?"

"Uh, can't see. Should we drop a log?" said his wingman, asking if they should light a flare.

"Hold off. Hang on. Fuck."

Doberman yanked his stick back with all his weight, just barely pulling off the ground as a heavy gust of wind kicked against the wings. Paying attention to the windscreen instead of his instruments, he'd inadvertently dropped too low. Flying a Hog in the dark wasn't necessarily difficult, but you had to pay attention to what you were doing.

He circled south of the two trucks and the damaged airplane, the altimeter nailed on three hundred feet above ground level. Devil Four was circling several thousand feet above and slightly to the south.

The players were getting hard to see. A flare might be a good idea.

Except it would help the Iraqis find their guys.

One of the trucks fired its machine gun, the stream of bullets arcing across the desert as Doberman passed. He rolled the Hog and sailed into what amounted to a 165-degree turn, pushing the wings out level as he got the nose angled onto the shadow. He lost speed and altitude—he was maybe ten feet off the ground when he put his nose on his target. Devil Three didn't seem to mind, though, nor did she complain when he kicked the Avenger 30mm Gatling back into action, a full three-second burst obliterating the tiny stream of machine-gun fire that was now aimed directly at his face.

Something scraped against his belly as he let off the trigger. For a moment Doberman thought he actually did hit the ground—he was very, very low. But as he pulled past the smoked target, he realized it must have been bullets from the Iraqi striking the Hog's titanium armor.

If they'd done any damage, the emergency lights weren't admitting it. All systems were in the green.

"Saved the best for last," said Gunny. "You nailed a tank. T-54, looks like. Opened him up like a can opener."

"Three," said Doberman. He'd flailed back at the target so fast he hadn't even known what he was hitting.

"Thanks, Yanks!" shouted a voice over the emergency rescue band. It was Sister Sadie's pilot.

"Devil Three to Sadie. We're a little confused on your position. Is that you near the plane?"

"Quite," responded the pilot. "Nav's back where we started. I had to retrieve a souvenir."

Doberman shook his head. Goddamn Brits were worse than Hog drivers.

"Stay put, would you?" Doberman told him. "We have to smoke the rest of the Iraqis so the helicopters can come in."

"It's a starlit night and I feel all right," sang the voice, laughing as if it were karaoke night. "But I've company."

"What the fuck are you saying?"

"More lorries down here," said the Brit, his voice only marginally more serious.

"Yeah, whatever. Stay out of the cross fire, okay?"

Lorries? Did he mean trucks?

Goddamn Brits couldn't even speak English.

20

Hawkins tried to control his anger as he unfolded the paper map over the hump of controls between the two pilots at the front of the Chinook. The SAS sergeant slapped his small flashlight twice without getting the light to work.

"Fuckin' shit ass," muttered the sergeant.

Hawkins reached into his pocket and got his own.

"We're here," he said, pointing. "Sadie's crew is about here."

"Further south, and they're busy," said the pilot, pointing to the side glass. Flashes lit the horizon.

If they were going to hit the base, they had to get moving. The Apaches were now one short and well into their fuel reserve, and even with the planned behind-the-lines refuel, they'd be pushing things. The Hogs too must be nearing their limit.

But he couldn't take the risk of flying the helicopters anywhere near serious antiair defenses.

Which, basically, was what Preston was concerned about, even if the shithead hadn't spelled it out.

He didn't know the major, but he had worked with two of the pilots in the Hog package, Doberman and Shotgun. If those guys thought there was a problem, there must really be a problem.

Better to fail than never to try.

Unless failure meant twenty dead men.

"Our chaps," said Sergeant Burns.

"They're all our chaps," said Hawkins. "We're going to have to scrub."

"I agree," said the pilot.

Burns didn't say anything. Hawkins bent his head slightly, studying the SAS sergeant's face in the wash from the dimmed cockpit lights.

"Best thing," said the commando finally.

"Let's go grab the Tornado crew," Hawkins told the pilot. "Go for it."

"Wait!" The copilot put out his hand, touching Hawkins as he listened to a transmission over the headphones. "The A-10's say there's a second wave of vehicles approaching. They may light a flare. Looks like quite a snit," said the copilot.

"Get me the Apaches, and then Devil One," said Hawkins. "Plot that course but hold until it's clear."

21

Doberman swung back to the south, climbing steadily. Gunny in Devil Four completed the far end of a figure eight about a half mile ahead, still flying at six thousand feet.

"Three Iraqi pickups," Gunny told him over the squadron frequency. "Moving toward the wreckage. I can nail them with the Mavericks."

"Hold off," Doberman told him.

Using Mavericks on relatively soft targets like pickups was a bit of an overkill. Had Shotgun been his wingman, the response would have been along the lines of: "Going for the best bang for the buck," or "Spoken like a real tax-payer." But Gunny simply acknowledged.

"Devil Three, this is Devil One," said Preston over the squadron frequency. "What's your status?"

"Circling over the crew. Three Iraqi vehicles approaching, about a mile off, little more. There may be some ground troops near our guys. Can't tell."

"Flare?"

"Figure it'll help them more than us. More than the Brits."

"Concur. Can you take the pickups?"

"Shit, yeah."

"They're going to send the Apaches north to help out. Chinooks will stand by to pick up the boys a mile back," responded Hack. "Lay it out for the Apaches."

The way Hack said it, connecting the dots for him like he was an imbecile, pissed Doberman off. Preston was just a little too perfect and crisp, the kind of guy who never did any wrong and let you know it. He thought the rest of the world couldn't cross the street if he wasn't there to take its hand.

Doberman steamed while Hack read him the com frequency for Splash Leader—which of course he already had—and then reminded him he was getting close to bingo—which of course he already knew.

"Repeat, Devil Three?" asked Hawkins, the Splash commander, as he snapped on to their frequency.

"Need you to move exactly three point five miles north, precisely north, from your position," said Doberman, working it out in his head. "When you're ready, I'll have our boys give you a flare."

The Apache commander got a little pushy when he clicked on, saying they were less than three minutes from the battlefield and asking which vehicles he could take.

"None. They're all ours," snapped Doberman, pushing the Hog's wing over. "Finders keepers."

22

Captain Conrad played striker on the squadron soccer team, and while he was perhaps not the most gifted athlete in the RAF, he had a certain quality of persistence and stamina that translated into goals late in the game.

As it was late in the game now, he put his stamina to good use, running for all he was worth from the shadow of Sister Sadie as fresh gunfire erupted in the distance.

One of the vehicles the A-10 had hit earlier flashed with a fresh explosion as its gas tank caught fire. The noise caught him off guard, unsettling his balance and sending him face-first into the ground. Conrad dropped the tape and had to hunt for it on his hands and knees, patting down the desert but finding nothing but sand. He heard a roar and then loud secondary explosions; grappling in the dust, he heard the distinct thump of approaching helicopters. Then he felt a rush of air—the A-10 had returned to attack the vehicles, which were closer to him than he'd thought.

The plane descended so low that its bullets passed only

a few yards away, streaming in front of his eyes like a surgeon's laser beam excising a tumor. The desert shrieked as the American lit his weapon in three distinct, brief bursts. Dirt and smoke and grit filled Conrad's eyes. He threw his head down, rubbing his face with his sleeve; he managed to clear one eye and groped again for the tape. Finding it, he stood, running again toward the sound of the approaching helicopter.

A small flare shot upward. His mate, no more than a quarter mile away.

Something thick and dark shot between them.

Conrad stopped quickly. There were shadows all around; with the battle smoke, falling darkness, and swirling sand, he'd completely lost his bearings.

The A-10 danced above him, cannon roaring again.

He could hear a truck motor and the clicks of automatic rifle fire approaching. He thought he could see the moving shadow. Red glints pricked closer.

He waited for the Hog to hit the truck. But there were no geysers of burning metal, no secondary explosions.

Conrad dropped to his knees. He pulled his emergency radio out of his vest, but couldn't hear anything over the roar. He checked his settings, tried again, then tossed it down and fumbled for his flare gun. He fired a charge not skyward but at the vehicle. A hiss, a whoosh, the sound of glass smashing—but the truck kept coming.

He couldn't find another flare, tossed the gun, and lost the radio, but held on to the tape and ran to his right, the only direction where there weren't shadows. He smelled burning metal, and something like antifreeze.

Trucks. Right behind him.

For the first time since he'd come to the Gulf—for the first time ever in his twenty-six years—he realized there were limits to life, realities that had nothing to do with his abilities or strength or will. Heavy caliber bullets cut a swath ten feet away; the truck barreled on. Conrad willed himself to his feet, pushing to the right, resigned to go out the way a soldier wanted to go out. He reached for his pistol, got it in his hand, and whirled around just in time to see the shadow of the Iraqi vehicle, an open-back Zil, crest a small hill less than ten yards away.

Then oblivion arrived.

But not for him. Red flames burst upward as the heavy fist of an A-10A Thunderbolt II smashed down on the Iraqi vehicle. The night tore in two as Conrad flew backward, propelled by some superhuman force that left him dazed and disoriented, but intact.

And with the video in his hand. He managed somehow to get back on his feet, realized he had both eyes open now, though they hurt like hell. He couldn't hear. His body seemed to feel the swirl of the battle continuing. Wind, sand, cordite, blood flew into his face.

Something fluttered a few yards away. A heli.

No, it was a wolf, snapping for him.

More like an Apache war bird, her Gat swiveling beneath her chin, so close it could poke him in the chest.

Conrad threw himself over the helicopter's right skid. "Go!" he yelled. "Go! Go!"

And it did, skittering backward a moment, twisting its body, then running a half mile south to a calmer place where the others were waiting and where Conrad, back to himself, began laughing hysterically as two burly SAS men pried him off the rail and hustled him to safety.

23

Part of him wanted to be philosophical—sometimes things went this way, all to hell.

But another part—a bigger part, a part that had driven Horace Gordon Preston to excel in school, in sports, in the Air Force—couldn't accept defeat, or even its hint. Horace Gordon Preston couldn't abide failure. And that part made him look for a way to salvage something, to find something to banish the taste if not erase the memory of things going to shit.

That was the reason, the only reason, he thought of the Roland launcher when the AWACS controller told him that the Weasel had failed to knock it out.

Logic argued against attacking it. The SAM system completely overmatched the A-10 and its operators had already proven they knew how to use it.

But logic didn't count for much, especially after Hawkins's disgusted tone when he agreed the mission had to be scrubbed.

A tone that had implied it was Preston's fault.

Delta dickwad.

Back less than a week with a Hog squadron, and he was already cursing as bad as any of them.

"Two, I want you to follow me down to seventy-five feet," Hack told Shotgun.

"Roger that," replied Shotgun, without even asking what their course heading was.

Maybe O'Rourke had read his mind. In any event, Hack was grateful that his wingman didn't question his judgment as he pushed his plane into the howling wind and tipped northeast, vectoring for the Roland's position. When he passed through five hundred feet the wind increased exponentially, and the Maverick-heavy Hog's airspeed dropped below two hundred knots. He pushed still lower, aiming to get under the Roland radar, falling through four hundred, three hundred, two hundred. The wind whipped up in a fury so intense that the plane moved straight downward at one point, dropping another fifty feet in a second. And then miraculously, inexplicably, everything went silky smooth. Preston eased his grip on the stick as the altimeter nailed fifty feet, airspeed climbing back toward three hundred miles an hour.

At night, in the dark, even over flat terrain, three hundred miles an hour feels incredibly fast when you are less than a hundred feet off the ground. Shadows leap up at you, hands try to pull you down to earth. The Hog lacked terrain-following radar; the only night-vision equipment at Hack's disposal was the IR seeker on the Maverick, which offered a very limited view. His knowledge of what lay ahead was based on a relatively primitive map that experience had shown was not always one hundred percent precise, and his sense of where exactly he was relied heavily on a navigation system proven to be less than one hundred percent reliable. Logic would have, should have, sent him home. But logic no longer had a place in Horace Gordon Preston's cockpit. He slammed the throttle to max as he neared the crunch zone, dividing his attention as evenly as possible among

he RWR, the windscreen, and the Mav's display, which
hosted several buildings, a road, more buildings, but no
SAMs.

"Zeus on your right," warned Shotgun, and the next in-
tant the sky filled with a stream of tracers, a hose of red
ire splurting about two o'clock off his nose. "Mine."

Something clicked in Hack's brain and he nudged the
Hog gently, pitching her on her axis to bring her path
slightly west as Shotgun fired an AGM at the gun, whose
errant fire was obviously optically aimed. Hack looked to
he Maverick screen, saw a series of buildings and the edge
of the river, then lost everything momentarily, the optical
sensor jangling for some unknown reason.

When the screen flashed back, Preston saw a low-slung
chassis shape in the upper right-hand corner. He slid the
cursor over and clicked his trigger to fire.

He hadn't locked on the Roland, however. He'd gotten
a small armored car.

A boneheaded, freshman-nugget, idiotic, deadly mistake. Because there was the Roland, bigger, hotter, on the
left. There was a flare and a launch—the missile operator
firing the missile blind.

Not blind, exactly, just without ground guidance. The
Roland was fully capable of finding its own target once
launched, and if its kill probability wasn't nearly as high in
manual mode, it was deadly nonetheless. Hack cursed
himself, hitting flares and chaff, kicking right quickly, trying to outrun the fire that suddenly ignited in his stomach.
Gravity punched him in the chest and pushed at his neck,
and a voice deep inside told him it served him right for
being such a fuckup, for not having what it took—for
choking when it was all on the line.

He zigged left, right, felt the missile piss through its
first stage, go terminal—he felt it reach for him, then
saw it, or saw something anyway, a large black shadow
that miraculously sailed right over his head and kept
going.

Then the ground exploded almost below him. Devil
One bucked, then shot clear, her nose pointing due south.

"I'm on your six," said Shotgun. "Splash one slightly used missile launcher. I'm thinking the Brits owe us big-time. You figure they stock Watney's, or are we going to have to settle for Bass?"

PART TWO

LOVERS

1

Every conceivable chore done, paperwork in order, contingencies prepared for, Lieutenant Colonel Michael Knowlington stood up from his desk and took a laboriously long, slow breath, filling his lungs from bottom to top with the recirculated Saudi air. He exhaled the breath twice as slowly as he had taken it in, pushing the air gently from his lungs, pushing until his stomach muscles flexed far toward his back.

Then he picked up the phone and, still standing, called his commanding general.

I want to resign, he planned to say.

Or, *I'm resigning.*

Or, *I'm quitting.*

Or, *I'm unfit for duty.*

His mind flitted back and forth among the possibilities, unsettled. The exact choice didn't matter; what was important was to hold his voice calm and to speak distinctly, and to get it started. He waited for the connection to be made, waited in the static limbo where he'd been since the flight took off to support Splash this afternoon.

"General is at dinner," said an aide's voice, breaking through the white noise.

"Excuse me?" said Knowlington, though he'd heard clearly.

"Not sure precisely when the general will back," said the aide. "Can I help you with something, sir?"

"No," said Skull.

"I can have him call you."

"That would be fine."

"Is it urgent?"

"It's important," Knowlington said, carefully choosing the word.

"He'll get back to you, Colonel."

Still standing in front of his desk, Michael Knowlington hung up the phone.

He'd spent his entire adult life in the Air Force. What would he do now? Take up one of the countless offers from old cronies to take a cushy job with a contractor?

Why not? Good money. Free booze.

He wouldn't drink. He couldn't stand it.

Who was he kidding? It took everything now not to bolt for the Depot.

He stared down at the phone. He should talk to his sisters, tell them.

He'd have to tell them sooner or later. He'd probably have to stay with one of them—Susan probably; Debbie was always busy with her kids.

He called Debbie, surprised that he got a line, surprised to hear the phone ring, surprised to hear her on the other end.

"Michael. It's about time you called," she said, as if she'd been waiting for him all day. "I've been thinking of you."

"Yeah?"

"I ran into Simona yesterday." His sister laughed. "She was talking about her son Jimmy wanting to be a pilot. I told her you would talk him out of it, of course."

Another time, he might have laughed. He'd gone out with Simona way back in high school, knew her now only as a vague acquaintance. She had two kids; Jimmy was the youngest. Her husband—what the hell did he do? Accountant or something for a large corporation. Kept track of toilet-paper orders for factories all across America.

"You'd be surprised, she's lost a lot of weight," said Debbie. "She looks a lot younger. I mean, we all look old."

"I'm coming home," Michael told his sister, the words rushing out.

He saw her push her head back, narrow her eyes, consider how to respond. She ran her hand through her light reddish-brown hair, put the phone back to her ear. He hadn't seen her in months, but he saw her clearly before him, felt her in the room.

"What's wrong, Michael?"

"I'm letting people down."

She understood the code as well as he did, knew what it referred to without having to use the words.

"So you're going to quit?"

Her voice, her face—as cold as their mother's. Colder.

"I don't want to hurt these kids."

"And you wouldn't be hurting them by quitting?"

"I'm not quitting." He paused, looking around the room, as if the explanation were a notice or bulletin tacked to the wall. "I can't trust myself."

She pressed her lips together, ran her fingers back through her hair. She'd have nothing more to say, would stand there in her kitchen, waiting for him to change the subject.

So he did.

"How's Bobby?" he said, asking after his nephew. He turned and sat on the edge of the desk.

"Growing like a weed. Jack wants to take him hunting, but I say no."

"Isn't it out of season?"

"Maybe." She gave a forced, self-deprecating laugh. "I'm not really sure how that works."

"Chris okay?"

"She may make valedictorian."

"Smart girl."

"Very."

"Well, I have to get going here."

"Michael—"

"I love you too," he said, though he knew that wasn't what she was going to say. "I'll be talking to you."

Knowlington slipped the phone back onto its cradle. It was all too much. He had to get a drink.

He hunched his shoulders and opened the door, moving quickly into the hallway. He ignored the framed photos slightly off-kilter on the wall—pictures of old war birds in their prime: a Mustang, the original Thunderbolt, a toothy Tomahawk, two different Phantoms, and a Sabre. He pulled open the door and trotted down the steps outside, resigned to his fate.

"Colonel Knowlington, a word, sir," snapped Captain Wong, materializing at his side just as he hit his stride.

Skull nearly jumped back, surprised by the intelligence specialist.

"Wong, what the hell are you doing?"

"Coming to get you on a matter of some urgency."

"I have to tell you, Captain, I'm really not in a mood for joking tonight."

"I'm not in the habit of making jokes, sir."

Wong. His voice was so distressed, so sincere, so straight, Knowlington couldn't help but laugh.

"You're a first-class ball-buster," he told the captain. "Shit, Wong, what the hell? What's up?"

"I'd like you take a look a picture," said the captain. "It's not very high quality, but I believe you would be extremely interested in its subject."

"*Its subject.* You crack me up," said Skull, pointing the captain back in the direction of his office.

2

Hack collapsed into the chair of the borrowed office at KKMC, sighing now that he was finally alone after a tedious and largely pointless debriefing with three different intelligence specialists in the base commander's office suite down the hall. His body felt like it had been pummeled by a dozen heavyweights. What wasn't bruised was cramped into jagged slabs of slate; his neck and shoulder muscles had more knots in them than a Persian rug.

One of the debriefers, a weasely looking Army guy from the CinC's staff, had implied that Hack wasn't aggressive enough. Hack had kept his cool, his Pentagon training coming to the fore—he hinted displeasure without making it absolutely explicit, emphasizing the "fluidity of the combat situation" in a way that strongly implied his guys had put their necks out damn far, thank you very much. The jerk finally nodded and left.

Of course, the Air Force guys implied just the opposite, wondering why the hell they'd gone for the Roland. Neither seemed terribly impressed when Shotgun said, "Because it was there," and walked out in exasperation.

Preston had been seriously tempted to join him. They'd saved the Tornado crew, killed a potent SAM site. They ought to get pats on the back, not questions.

The Army guy truly boiled him. What the hell else did he expect?

But what did Hack expect of himself? He felt, he knew, he'd screwed up a couple of times today, big-time.

Preston shifted uneasily in the chair, trying to position his legs so the cramps might ease. Still technically on alert for Splash, Devil Squadron had been loaned the small, nondescript room as temporary operational headquarters, rest area, and bus station. The furnishings included four metal folding chairs, a very lopsided card table, and an empty footlocker that looked and smelled as if it dated from World War I.

Gunny and Doberman were catching some Zs in a "guest" building across the way. They had to prep a separate assignment at 0400; at least as far as Hack was concerned, they were no longer part of the operation. Shotgun had gone in search of real coffee, claiming Dunkin' Donuts had set up a franchise near the mosque not far from the hangar area.

It might very well be true. Guys didn't call KKMC the Emerald City for nothing. The massive mosque and fancy buildings surrounding the airstrip enhanced the Las Vegas image. They were close to Iraq and Kuwait, but this wasn't the usual austere forward operating area. If there was Dunkin' Donuts coffee anywhere in the Gulf, it'd be here. And if there was Dunkin' Donuts, Shotgun would find it.

Hack realized his legs were only going to get stiff sitting down. He got up and began pacing the room. He probably ought to just bag it and go get some sleep. The Splash mission would definitely be called off; no way they'd go ahead with it now that the Iraqis knew they were interested in the base.

On the other hand, it might take the Iraqis a while to reinforce the place. They *might* be scared shitless to move during the night, with American bombers in such absolute control. Or maybe they would *only* move at night, and have to wait until orders came from Saddam in the morning.

No way to know, no way to predict. The Spec Ops and SAS wizards were cooking it all up in their pot of stew right now. The backup had been to attack at dawn, so maybe it was on.

Preston stopped walking and did a few squats, legs creaking like those of an eighty-year-old trying to take the stairs in the nursing home.

A bleary-eyed Air Force lieutenant appeared at the door. "Major Preston?" he asked.

Hack rose from his squat sheepishly. "That's me."

"Delta and the SAS want to set up a talk at 2400, sir. They're arranging a satellite slot."

Great, thought Hack—a conference call at midnight. He'd have to wait around now; no way he'd get back up in time if he took a nap.

"We'll handle the arrangements, sir," added the lieutenant. "Base commander's office will be available. You can come on down a few minutes beforehand. We'll make some extra-strength coffee," added the lieutenant, trying but failing to inject some cheer into his voice. Poor guy didn't look like he'd slept in weeks.

"Thanks, Lieutenant," said Hack. "I'll come looking for you if I need anything."

The lieutenant grimaced slightly as he smiled; it was obvious he hoped Hack wouldn't add to his workload.

As he walked from the room his shoulders sagged. Hack couldn't help but remember the advice one of his mentors had given him in the early days of his Pentagon assignment: Somebody piles more work on you than you can handle, smile and ask for more.

Then pass it off to someone else.

Obviously the lieutenant worked for someone who took the advice to heart.

Hack decided he might as well go find some real coffee, maybe see what O'Rourke was up to. As he stepped into the hallway, Major Preston heard the muffled strains of music. It happened to be coming from the direction of the building's foyer, or at least seemed to, growing louder as he walked. The notes strained unevenly; they came from a keyboard of some type, played by someone who didn't have much sense of tempo. The sound reminded Hack of some of his high school music classes. His band teacher had been a particularly poor keyboardist, but nonetheless went at it every day before class.

The music abruptly stopped as he reached the steps leading down to the front door. Hack noticed another small flight off to the right that led down to a well-lit hallway. Curious, he jogged down. There he spotted a black board with white letters announcing ecumenical Christian services.

Today was Sunday; he'd completely lost track.

Curious about the music and feeling a little guilty that he'd missed his first Sunday service in more than a year, Hack poked his head into the room. A preacher stood at a wooden lectern, reading from the Scripture to a scattered audience of six. The words immediately struck Preston— they were from Ecclesiastes, a section of the Bible his mother and grandmother had often cited when he was growing up. Hack had even pasted a line from a section of the biblical book to his flight board, a reminder to do what was wise and just, always.

Easy in theory, he thought, listening to the reverend. Difficult in reality, especially in war. Hack entered the room and sat in the last of the twelve rows. The empty chairs made the space seem cavernous. An electronic keyboard sat near the reverend's lectern; one of its stilt legs had been repaired with a thick tangle of duct tape.

"Who is the wise man? A man's wisdom makes his face shine, and the boldness of his face shall be changed." The minister nodded his head, pausing for effect.

But you couldn't tell who was wise and who wasn't by looking at his face, Hack thought. You couldn't guess what people were worth by looking at them. They changed.

Look at Knowlington—take him out of Washington, and the guy was actually wise, or damn close to it.

What about himself? Take him out of an F-15 and put him in an A-10 and he was worthless.

Worthless? Just because he'd flubbed the wind correction on his bombing run?

Or locked on an armored car instead of a missile launcher?

Or hadn't been aggressive enough? How much more aggressive could he have been? Aggressive enough to get shot down? What if the helicopters had been hit?

What was wisdom? What was folly?

The minister continued on, his thin voice as earnest as any Hack had ever heard. The man's eyes shone like faceted glass as he spoke, clearly lost in the advice he was giving.

Preston had listened to many sermons like this in his life, sometimes with rapt attention, more often with indifference as he daydreamed about something else. The minister's voice evoked something different in him tonight—he thought about how naive the reverend must be, how innocent of his surroundings.

He knew it wasn't fair. He also knew he ought to get up and find Shotgun, let him know what was going on with the mission. But he stayed listening, watching the reverend speak. He remained as the service ended and the others filed out. He was still sitting when the minister walked to the electronic keyboard and turned it off.

"Can I help you, son?" asked the minister, walking toward him.

"I'm as old as you, maybe older," Preston said.

The man laughed, nodding his head. "Age comes with the collar, I'm afraid. I saw you listening to the sermon."

"I have a line from Ecclesiastes on my flight board. I carry it with me every flight. Wisdom exceeds folly."

"It does."

"But you can't always tell what's wise, and what's just dumb."

The reverend bit his lower lip with his teeth, nodding

his head slowly. The lids of his eyes squeezed together slightly, as if he were considering the quote for the first time. "I think that may be the point of the passage," he said finally.

"No," said Hack. "I don't think so. No one ever said that," he added, thinking of all the discussions he'd heard.

"Maybe they were wrong?"

"You think what we're doing here is right? I mean, we could be fooling ourselves and wouldn't know it."

Hack felt his throat contract as the words ran out of his mouth. He hadn't meant to say anything like that—he hadn't been consciously thinking of that, and even if he had, he'd never raise the question with a stranger, not even one who was a minister.

He stood, surprised at himself, a little embarrassed even, waiting for the reverend to reassure him, to say something like: "Of course it's right, justice must be done."

It was the sort of thing chaplains tended to say. But this one looked at him and said nothing for a moment.

"I don't know. Honestly, I'm not sure," said the reverend finally. "I struggle with it. To see someone die must be a horrible thing."

"I've never actually seen anyone die," said Hack. "But I have killed a man. Or probably I did. I shot down a MiG."

"Does it weigh on your conscience?"

"No. It doesn't," he said honestly. "I hadn't really thought of it. Not in that way. Not that I killed someone."

How did he think of it? He thought of it as a contest, a game almost.

No. As a job. Like the one he'd had in high school, cutting grass. Something he had to do.

Surely the other pilot would have killed him if he had the chance. Did that make it right, or wise?

Why had he held back on the Splash mission?

He hadn't held back at all. Screw the Army briefer, screw Hawkins, screw anyone who suggested that. His guys saved two men's lives and that was worth something, no matter what you measured it against.

"It is a struggle, deciding what is wise and what is folly," agreed the minister. "Would you like to get a drink?"

"A drink?" Hack laughed. "No."

"Ministers drink."

"I know that," Preston said. "But I have a, uh, a kind of thing I have to do." Splash was top secret and he couldn't give any details. "I'm on standby."

"Oh," said the chaplain, clearly disappointed. "Coffee?"

"Nah," said Hack. "Thanks anyway. Nice service."

3

BJ Dixon stared at the canvas ceiling of his tent, trying to remember what it felt like to fly. Wind rattled the fabric, a whispery hush that made it seem as if he'd fallen into a void. He couldn't remember how to fly—he could barely remember how to walk. The yellow air of the tent pressed against his chest like Iraqi dirt; the rumbles in the distance were the groans of men dying, of the grenade exploding in the little boy's stomach.

"BJ?"

He turned his head toward the door.

"Lieutenant?"

Dixon sat up and swung his bare feet off the cot. He had on dress uniform pants; they were the only pants clean enough to wear. Cold, he'd layered all four of his clean T-shirts over his chest.

"It's okay," he said.

Becky Rosen slid slowly inside, holding the door open only far enough to let her slender body through.

"I saw your light," she said.

"Can't sleep," BJ told her.

"I—" She shrugged.

"What?"

"I was wondering how you were, after everything up there."

"Okay. Cold."

"I heard you were going home."

"No." He folded his arms around his chest, a wave of cold air hitting him. "They said I could. I don't feel like it. I want to be here."

She nodded. "Get right back on the horse? Fly again?"

"It seems like it's been forever since I flew, you know?"

"Those your dress pants?"

"Yeah." He laughed—briefly, barely, but still, it was a laugh. "Nothing else is clean."

"I know the feeling."

They'd kissed once, in the dark, by accident really. Her lips had been warmer and deeper and softer than anything he'd ever felt. But it had been so long ago now, before he had known anything, before going north, before the kid.

Rosen shifted her body, her head moving backward. Dixon realized he didn't want her to leave, but could think of nothing to get her to stay.

"You were in Iraq?" he blurted out. Wong had told him about the mission she'd volunteered for.

"Yes." She laughed, a tiny little laugh. "I parachuted in with Captain Wong. He's some sort of skydiving special-ist. A regular James Bond."

"Saved my life," said Dixon.

"Thank God." She flexed her fingers, rubbing them to-gether. He'd never seen anything so beautiful.

"Cold in here," he said.

"Really? I feel warm."

"Yeah." He worked his tongue around his dry mouth, trying to work up some moisture. "It was so cold in Iraq, I'm still frozen."

"You're a hero." The words were blurted out.

"Nah."

"That helicopter you shot down."

"That was luck."

"And then you saved that sergeant's life. I saw that ridge and the quarry you were in. It must've been hell."

"You saw that?"

"I was in one of the helicopters. The AH-6. Captain Wong didn't tell you?"

"No."

"Yeah, I was."

"Yeah," he repeated. His head became hollow again; he remembered climbing along the rock face, the wind rushing around his body as he waited for his chance to kill a man—three men as it turned out, one with his bare hands.

"They wouldn't have, they wouldn't have sent you to Iraq if they, they didn't think you were—brave," said Rosen.

Her words jerked him back to the present, to her.

"I got tangled up with Delta on my own," he said. "Ground FAC. I volunteered. I ended up working with Captain Glenon and Shotgun."

"Captain Glenon saved us, our helicopter, at Fort Apache."

"Good guy."

Rosen's cheeks turned red. She said nothing. Surprised, Dixon looked at her, waiting for her eyes to glance upward from the floor. He hadn't thought she liked Doberman, not that way at least.

He'd thought, in fact, that she liked *him*.

She must. Otherwise, why was she here?

"Was it bad?" she asked.

He wanted to tell her about the boy. He saw the boy and he saw the grenade as he began to speak. But instead of telling her about the kid, instead of talking about Iraq and the howl in his head and how much he'd forgotten and how bad his stomach hurt, his tongue found a different story altogether.

"My mother died about a year ago, a little more now," said Dixon. His head seemed to pull back from the words, as if they were physical things filling the air between them. "I sat by her side for a long time, just waiting."

The words stopped. Rosen nodded, then stared at him.

Nothing else had ever been so beautiful.

"I better go," she said abruptly, turning for the door.

He caught her arm. The biceps was harder than he expected, a thick tree branch.

"Don't," he said.

The kiss was softer, way softer, than he'd expected, and way longer than he could have hoped.

4

"The hangar roof makes positive identification difficult, admittedly," Wong told Colonel Knowlington. "And the enhancement technique that has been applied to the original infrared rendering has been known to distort images under similar circumstances. Nonetheless, the pitot head at the nose confirms the identification. It is a MiG-29. No other plane in the Iraqi inventory would cast such a shadow."

Skull took the paper and put it less than an inch from his eyes, trying to distinguish the black shadow from the rest of the black shadows on the thermal-print paper. The image had started as an infrared videotape of the Splash airfield taken by the Tornado shortly before it was shot down. British intelligence had analyzed and enhanced the picture with a computer program that could separate objects of different primary heat characteristics—in other words, find objects hidden beneath tarps or, in this case, thinly roofed buildings. According to Wong, the aircraft had either been recently flown, or had been heated by the exposure of a day's worth of sun before being moved into the relatively small hangar building at the Splash airfield. Since it definitely hadn't been there yesterday, it must've recently arrived.

Skull saw only a vague and dark arrow inside a gray rectangle.

"You might prefer viewing this image," said Wong, removing another sheet from his folder. This was an even blurrier photocopy of the same general area, with a portion outlined in fine red pen.

Granted, the outline looked somewhat like the outline of a MiG-29.

Or an F-15. Or a chipped piece of slate.

"It is an aircraft, I assure you," said Wong, as if reading Knowlington's mind. "And it was flown, or at least exposed to the sun, within the past eight hours."

"But why would they put it there?" Skull asked.

"I can think of several reasons. The simplest would be to hide it, hoping that the base had been overlooked. It would be easier to get it there than Iran."

Several Iraqi fighters had scrambled to Iran over the past several days, possibly for safekeeping, though it wasn't entirely clear why they had gone or what they intended on doing. The Iranians had claimed the planes would be interred, but no one entirely trusted them.

"Maybe they're staging to Iran," suggested Skull.

"Possible, though once in the air their modus operandi has been to continue east."

"Mechanical problems?"

"Possibly, though again, I can think of much better places to land."

"Maybe they're going to plumb it for bombs and send it south."

Wong nodded grimly. "The so-called Death Wish scenario cannot be ruled out. It would not be difficult to adapt the plane for use as a bomber, especially if the mission were one-way. There are other developments that indicate this plane may fly again, very soon."

The captain pulled out another sheet of paper from his folder. A satellite image taken around dusk, it was even darker than the Tornado pictures.

"The truck here arrived after the overflight, perhaps a few minutes before this was taken. It appears to be in motion, in fact, though that is difficult to tell here," said Wong.

"What truck?" asked Knowlington.

Wong pointed to a black curlicue near the runway, which itself was barely discernible. "In this revetment. It is a tanker, and while it could carry any number of liquid cargoes, my best guess would be aviation fuel for the jet."

"You see a fuel truck there?"

"The limitations of the available technology," said Wong, sighing with regret. "But yes, that is what that is."

"Well, if that's a fuel truck, the plane may be gone already."

"Possibly. But a night mission would be hazardous, and perhaps beyond the capabilities of both the plane and the pilot. Additionally, the airstrip is very short, even for a MiG-29. It's unlit, and the falloff at the very end of the runway, combined with the nearby hills, makes the takeoff tricky."

"None of that would be critical," said Skull.

"I can't argue decisively," agreed Wong. "But as the fuel truck is in the revetment, not the hangar area, the soonest I would positively anticipate takeoff would be dawn."

"Maybe they're still working on the jet," suggested Knowlington. "Maybe it had engine trouble and set down."

"Possibly. It is not obvious from the intelligence. There are no indications of work crews, at least at present. There are several bunkers nearby, however, which could house any type of weapon."

"You think they're going to use it to bomb Riyadh?"

"The permutations are endless," said Wong. "In my personal opinion, it is more likely that the plane will join others in a dash to Iran, or simply remain at the base. But the aircraft's present location and the relative lack of defensive assets present a unique opportunity for intelligence gathering."

Skull reexamined the images. "These pictures are pretty lousy, Wong."

"My intention is to gather intelligence firsthand."

"You want to go in with Splash. That's what you're saying?"

"It would be convenient."

Skull scowled. "We have to bomb this sucker right away. It's an easy target."

"CentCom has already been alerted to the presence of the aircraft, and it can be interdicted if it flies south. My suggestion is that the Splash team destroy it as part of the operation to search for the missing SAS men. Prior to destroying the aircraft, a brief interlude of inspection would confirm or contradict a number of theories regarding not only the plane but the state of the Iraqi Air Force. It would also add considerably to our store of knowledge regarding Soviet-export MiGs. It is an opportunity, frankly, that one such as myself cannot afford to miss." Wong folded his arms in front of his chest. "I have already arranged for a UH-1 to transport me to the area where the Splash team is spending the night. With your permission, I will leave within the hour."

"And what if I don't give you permission?"

Wong's head snapped upright. Skull had the impression it was the first thing he had said that Wong hadn't already considered.

Knowlington realized that Wong could easily go around him if he chose; the intelligence officer was here only on temporary duty, and ultimately reported directly to an admiral in the Pentagon responsible for Joint Service Intelligence. Wong was considered one of the West's leading experts on Russian weapons systems, and had dozens of covert actions and spy missions to his credit; this one would hardly seem outrageous.

"What about the SAS men who are supposed to be prisoners here?" Skull asked.

"As I noted earlier, I doubt the Iraqis would hold them here," said Wong. "But it cannot be ruled out. Baghdad might have them placed here until a proper decision on how to best exploit or at least hold them was made; we cannot tell. At the same time, a unit commander deciding to exploit them for political gain or favor with the regime might indeed keep them at an out-of-the-way base while he contemplated the best way to capitalize on their presence. The base appears to be outside the Iraqis' normal chain of command, or at least is not home to a large contingent of men."

"Makes sense, I guess."

"Only in Iraq," said Wong. "In any event, my inspection of the plane need not interfere with the search for the men, which would remain the primary objective. With your permission, Colonel."

Skull turned his head toward the phone. He expected it to ring any second—expected to end his responsibilities within the hour, if not minutes.

Until then?

Giving permission to Wong was a no-brainer. The danger was clearly outweighed by the information that would be gained.

Was it, though? They knew plenty about MiG-29's, and the Iraqi Air Force had been a no-show to this point in the war. Sending a guy across the border wasn't exactly the same as asking him to run down to the 7-Eleven for a gallon of milk.

"You think this is worth the risk?" Skull asked Wong.

The intelligence expert sighed in the manner of a physics teacher asked once more to explain the relevance of $E=MC^2$.

"Since the operation will go ahead in any event, the additional risk is infinitesimal. Obtaining firsthand information on the plane would be beneficial. There are the obvious questions of what changes if any have been made to the weapons systems and whether it has been adapted for ground attack. And then there are the more interesting queries. Has the full N-019 radar set, the so-called Slot Back 1, actually been installed? Has the cannon—"

Knowlington put up his hand, stopping what promised to be a long list. "All right. Go for it. You sure you don't want to take a flatbed up there with you and haul it home?"

"That would be preferable," said Wong. "In fact—"

"I'm kidding. Jesus, you're a ball-buster. Have you told Hawkins?"

"I planned to do so after consulting with you," said Wong. "There is an additional consideration for the Splash mission inherent in the presence of the aircraft. Regardless of whether the SAS men are being kept at the base or not, if the plane is there, and even more so if it is planning an actual attack, point defenses will be moved in, certainly in response to the Tornado overflight. We should expect a half-dozen ZSU-23 chassis, and perhaps a lower-grade missile system. Indeed, I believe at least one SA-9 launcher has been reported en route, though I have not been able to coordinate the intelligence."

The SA-9 was a short-range surface-to-air missile; while it posed more of a risk to helicopters than Maverick-bearing Hogs, it would have to be dealt with.

"We'll have to tell Hack. It might be a stretch for two planes to hit all the guns and missiles besides," added Skull. "Doberman and Gunny have a mission at 0600, so they're coming out of the package."

"I would say four planes are the minimum needed to support the mission—more would be optimum."

The hangar should be targeted by one of the Hogs. If anything went wrong, a Maverick could obliterate the MiG, whatever Saddam's plans.

To arrange for four planes, he'd have to go himself. There simply wasn't another experienced pilot available who could lead such a hazardous mission.

No?

No.

He hesitated, remembering the idea that had occurred to him earlier, the cloud of 23mm slugs enveloping him.

His own death wish?

Knowlington glanced at the old-style phone on his desk. At any second its ring might change everything.

"All right, let's get on this," Skull told Wong. "Set up satellite time with the SAS and whoever else needs to be clued in. I'll deal with the British command, and I'll rejigger the duty rosters and find two other planes and pilots."

"Understood," said Wong.

Aware that he was moving a bit too fast but unable to slow down, Knowlington jumped from his chair and ran from the room, out of the telephone's reach.

5

"Have you a cigarette?"

Captain Hawkins jumped up from the tire of the howitzer carriage where he'd been sitting, staring over the sandbags at the approaching shadow.

"Startled you?" asked Sergeant Burns, his face finally visible in the dark night.

"A little," admitted Hawkins.

"Cigarette?"

"Don't smoke."

The SAS sergeant leaned against the gun, next to Hawkins. "I do. Have one."

"No, thanks."

"Not even tempted?"

"No."

"English cigarettes don't cause cancer," said the sergeant. He snorted, then clicked open a metal lighter. An odor of lighter fluid mingled with the smoke as he lit up.

"You did the right thing," Burns told him. "Calling it off."

Hawkins shrugged.

"Pilot has two kids."

Everybody has someone, Hawkins thought. But he said nothing.

"Have another go at dawn?"

"I'd like to, yeah," Hawkins told the Englishman. "Assuming your guys haven't found them yet. We won't know until close to midnight. I've arranged for a phone conference."

"Ring 'em up," said the sergeant, exhaling. "Ring 'em up."

Hawkins wasn't quite sure what he meant, or even what he might want. Probably just wanted to shoot the shit for a while.

The Delta captain sat down again on the trailer, shuffling his feet in the sand. The artillery base was a few miles from Iraq, used more for staging and supply than actual bombardment, though of course that could change in an instant. The team had been given a trio of bunkers to sack out in not far from the makeshift airfield where the helicopters were being serviced.

They'd be ready for another "go" by 0400, assuming the Brits gave the green light. His men would be tired, but so would the Iraqis. There wouldn't be a last-second flyby this time, but he'd have the benefit of the latest satellite data as well as the Tornado intelligence, which he'd already seen.

Damn blurry copy of a blurry image. The pilot and his crewman had been airlifted to an RAF base; the video images had been processed and several faxed to Hawkins. As far as he could tell, there were still no serious defenses, beyond the antiair artillery that had been there before.

"I'm a family man myself," said the sergeant. "Don't look it, I know," he added. "Five kids, though. Five shiny faces. Had to join the squadron just for peace."

"You have five kids?" asked Hawkins.

"Almost a football team." The sergeant took a long

draw on his cigarette. "Took the family to Blackpool just before we came. Adventure."

The SAS commando began recounting the trip to the amusement park, which sounded to Hawkins like the English equivalent of Coney Island, only better. There was a mammoth roller coaster there, supposedly the highest in the world. Cars reached eighty-five miles an hour on the downhill.

"Scared shitless, I don't mind saying. Nearly threw up right in the seat. Did on the ground," said the sergeant. "Scariest thing I ever did."

"Scarier than this?"

"Oh, much. Scarier than Belfast, and I served there eighteen months. And Londonderry."

"I have relatives there."

"Oh." He sucked the cigarette down to its filter. "Catholic, I imagine."

"That's right."

"Humph," said the sergeant. He threw the cigarette down, took out another. "Hard life, that."

"Probably is."

Burns lit his cigarette. He shifted his weight, but didn't move off the big gun. "I expect we'll get the go."

"I hope so," said Hawkins.

"Went on that roller coaster three times in a row," said the sergeant. "Didn't want the kiddies to see I was scared. Turned the stomach inside out, that."

"I imagine it would." Hawkins laughed. "I don't like roller coasters myself."

6

Rebecca Rosen floated in a pool of warm water, her body still shaking from making love with BJ. It hadn't been what she'd thought—it was better, better, better. Her head vibrated; she'd fallen away from time, away from the war. The world outside no longer existed. Reality was here, on this tiny cot, BJ's body pressed gently against hers, his face leaning against her breast, his breath brushing back and forth across her neck. His eyes were closed; she drifted toward sleep as well, lost, pleasantly, lusciously lost, finally oblivious to the aches and distresses of life.

But the world was a hard master.

"Knock, knock," said a voice from beyond the bubble surrounding her.

"Knock, knock"—part-mocking, part-smirking, part-warning, part-censoring . . .

Colonel Knowlington entered the tent, standing over them. BJ jumped up, pulling the blankets with him to cover up. Rosen rolled over, belatedly hiding her face. She considered diving to the floor, but didn't dare.

"Lieutenant, I need you as a backup for Splash," said Knowlington to Dixon sharply. "I need you on the runway no later than 0400. You'll fill in if somebody gets sick. I'll brief you at 0230. Good night."

The tent shook as the colonel turned sharply on his heel and left without acknowledging her presence or nakedness.

"Fuck," said Dixon.

Becky turned over, then slowly pulled her hands away from her eyes. She looked at him, pale and beautiful in the dim light of the tent. Then she began to laugh.

7

To be a first sergeant of any military organization is to be a philosopher. True, all first sergeants—all sergeants, period—are practical engineers, skilled in the sciences of organization and bureaucracy, to say nothing of bullshit. To reach the exalted level of master sergeant, a man—or woman—must master the twin arts of motivation and discipline; he—or she—must be more skilled at politics than any candidate for President. He—or she—must practice the art of war in a way that would humble Sun Tzu, though of course the best sergeants never need to fire a weapon, for the enemy retreats at the mere hint of their approach.

In a chief master sergeant, genius exerts itself without appearing to sweat. Procurement, persuasion, prophecy—no Greek god or goddess ever had half the attributes of a chief master sergeant, whose very grunt or growl could send an army to glorious victory.

But a *first* sergeant, a leader of men and minder of officers—a first sergeant also had to be a genius of thought, a translator of the ethereal and timeless. For who but a first sergeant could properly frame the unending questions of life? Who but a first sergeant could say, with a straight face and great authority, *This is this*? Who but a first sergeant could look at a glass and declare that it was neither half full nor half empty, but rather, a symbol of man's status in the universe.

And the best damn beer he'd quaffed in at least twenty-four hours.

"The best," repeated the capo di capo from the armchair in his oversized temp tent in the heart of Tent City.

"Better than that porter Elwell brought in from Czecho-slovakia," said Sergeant Melfi, sitting on the capo's right. Despite being a mere staff sergeant, Melfi showed great promise—but naturally the same could be said for all of the capo's handpicked minions.

"Czechs don't make porter," said Technical Sergeant Luce dismissively.

"I wouldn't say that," said Clyston. "Blanket statements like that will get you in trouble every time."

He took a long sip from his glass, savoring the bouquet. Since he was in a war zone, he limited himself to two beers each night, lingering far longer over each glass than he would in the States. But self-restraint sharpened the palate.

"As a general rule, Czech porter is not the best porter," said Luce, amending his pronouncement. "Now, you want to talk about pilsners—that's a whole different kettle of yeast."

Clyston snorted approvingly at Luce's turn of phrase. "Gentlemen, I believe it's time for a smoke," he said, reaching for the humidor below his chair. He opened it and removed a Cuban Partagas Lusitania, then offered the pol-ished walnut box to Melfi, who selected a Punch in the robusto size. Luce, as was his custom, passed.

They had just lit up when Aaron Racid, an E-4 ordnance loader or candyman, rushed into the tent without knock-ing—a violation of protocol so serious that it could only be caused by a crisis.

Which it was.

"Devereaux's sitting on a Maverick and won't get off," the weapons specialist told the capo. "Swear to God, Sarge. Lost his fucking mind. Lost his fuck-*ing* mind."

Clyston put down his beer and unfolded himself from the chair. "I'll be back," he told his men, stoking the flame of his double corona with a big puff before following Racid out to Oz.

Seven Hogs sat in various stages of dress in and around the hangars. The day's bombing runs had been relatively easy for the Devil Squadron, and none had been damaged or even nicked. With no major maintenance tasks and hours before most of the squadron needed to be at the flight line, only a light crew was on duty. The candymen were supposed to be loading up a pair of Hogs that Colonel Knowlington wanted to use to support a covert deep-strike mission. Racid's description of the problem had not been entirely accurate. Devereaux sat on *two* Mavericks, his butt on one and his legs on the other. Both missiles were on low-slung trolleys directly in front of Devil Five. Two other bomb loaders stood several feet away, throwing worried looks at Racid.

"Devereaux, what the F is going on?" said Clyston, looking not at Devereaux but the others. The men took half steps backward as he pulled his cigar from his mouth. "You guys find some coffee."

"Yes, Sergeant," they said in unison, disappearing.

Clyston turned toward Devereaux. The E-4 weighed at least 220 pounds. While the AGMs were safed and designed for semirough handling, it was never a good idea to treat any ordnance lightly, let alone as a couch.

"You resting?" Clyston asked.

"No, Sergeant."

"You intending on loading these?"

"I'd prefer not to."

Now in theory, there were a million ways to handle a situation like this. The sergeant could ask for a clarification of what the hell "prefer not to" meant. Or he could skip the bull, give a direct order, and wait for it to be fulfilled. If it wasn't—as seemed somewhat likely—he could on his own authority have Devereaux forcibly removed, even placed under arrest. Charges could be brought, or the man could be removed to medical care.

But the capo, mindful that the head on his perfect beer back at the tent was steadily dissipating, did not have time for anything so involved. He took a thoughtful puff on his cigar, and went to his ordie.

"Mind if I sit down?"

Devereaux shoved over slightly. Clyston gingerly placed himself on the Maverick next to him.

"Thinking of what these suckers can do, huh?"

Devereaux, who obviously had been doing just that, said nothing for a moment. Then he asked if the capo had ever heard Mozart's *Requiem*.

"I was just listening to it, as a matter of fact," said Clyston. He had long held that fibs in the line of duty were not fibs at all.

"Shows you how puny we are," said Devereaux.

"Not really," said Clyston. "Shows what man is capable of. Giving the angels a voice." He hummed a small piece from the overture—the sergeant did, in fact, have a recording of the masterwork in his tent, along with many of Mozart's other works.

Devereaux jerked his head around for a moment, then looked at the ground. "I don't want to kill anybody, Sergeant."

Funny how this kind of stuff never came up at the recruitment office. Clyston took a long puff on his cigar. One thing he had to give the Marxist bastard Castro—he sure as shit knew how to roll tobacco.

"I know I'm not pulling the trigger," continued Devereaux. "But no man's an island."

Donne and Mozart in the same conversation. Almost made flat beer worthwhile.

Maybe not, thought Clyston, reconsidering. Still, it was an elevated sort of conversation, not the type you usually had with a weapons guy. Bomb loaders as a class weren't generally given to classical music and poetry, unless you numbered the Beastie Boys among the great masters.

Clyston exhaled the smoke from his cigar.

"Fate's a funny thing," he told his airman. "Puts you places you never thought you'd be."

Devereaux nodded, then looked toward the sky. Clyston folded his left arm under his right, taking another long, slow drag on the cigar.

"Yeah. Fate," said the ordie. "Can't live with it. Can't live without it."

Now *that* was bomb-grunt philosophy.

Clyston savored a mouthful of smoke. "Damn straight," he said, blowing a perfect ring. "Damn straight."

"Excuse me, Sergeant," said the E-4, slipping his feet off the Maverick. "You don't mind, but I have to get these suckers loaded. And, uh, no offense, but this isn't the safest place to be smoking a cigar."

"Good point, Devereaux," said Clyston. "Carry on."

8

Hack pushed the receiver closer to his ear, trying to pick up the others through the static. There were more than a dozen British and American officers on the line, and all of them sounded as if they were underwater or had filled their mouths with sand.

"Neither Tension nor Hercules produced anything," said the British SAS major reviewing the search operations. "Light resistance, including some SAM activity, was encountered at both sites."

Hack took that as a slap, but kept his mouth shut as the major continued. The British RAF general ultimately responsible for the missing men had opened up the phone conference by tossing Devil Squadron a bone, saying that the two RAF fliers credited the Hogs with saving their skins. If anyone criticized Preston directly, he'd throw that back in their faces. In the meantime, it was best to keep quiet.

"Splash remains our only possibility," said the major

after detailing some other leads that had washed out. "Granted, it is still a long shot."

"Our team is intact," Hawkins interjected. "We never got to the base, and the helicopters were undetected. We're good to go."

Hack started to say that he and Shotgun were ready as well, but he was cut off by Captain Wong.

"The small base we are calling Splash may be more significant than original estimates surmised," said Wong.

It was obvious from the background noises that he was speaking from a helicopter, though he didn't bother to explain why he was aboard one, let alone how he managed the link. Wong launched into a long and somewhat muffled dissertation on what the tapes from the Tornado overflight and recent satellite photos showed. Unable to follow Wong amid growing static, Preston dug his nail into the Styrofoam coffee cup—real Dunkin' Donuts, as Shotgun had promised. As the unintelligible filibuster continued, Hack glanced at the box of doughnuts on the desk, which lay just out of reach. He considered putting the phone down and grabbing another Boston cream. As implausible as it seemed, the treats were authentic. O'Rourke could probably find a McDonald's in downtown Baghdad.

If Hack ever took command of the squadron, he'd make Shotgun one of the flight leaders. Not because of the doughnuts—the guy was a damn good pilot, a kick-ass pilot, even though personally he looked like a slob. Glenon—Glenon had too much of a temper to be a front-line jock, in Hack's opinion, though he obviously must do well in peacetime exercises and the like.

Wong—Wong could go back to the Pentagon or wherever he came from. He kept talking and talking, even though all he seemed to be saying was that there were now two very short-range missile launchers at Splash, SA-9's.

Preston gave into temptation and stretched for the doughnut. When he picked the phone back up, Wong was still detailing the point defenses, noting that four more trucks with antiair artillery had been seen on the road nearby. The SA-2 site they had identified earlier remained a potent threat, even though it had not come up during the aborted mission.

"They're probably defunct," said Preston harshly. "They're not a factor."

Despite his hope that that would cue someone else to take over the conversation, Wong kept right on talking.

"There is a building at garshawl eastern gergawsh."

Static descended over his words, scrambling the sentences as effectively as a 128-byte encryption key. The words Hack could make out sounded something like shadows inside a building, though that didn't make much sense.

"Hey, hold on," said Shotgun, practically shouting into his headset. Hack pulled the phone away from his ear quickly, but his eardrum felt like it had been shattered. "What you're saying is there's a plane in the hangar?"

"Affirmative," said Wong.

"What kind of plane?" asked Hack.

"That is what I intend to find out. I believe it is a MiG-29, variant unknown. My task will be to examine the plane and gather as much detail about it as possible."

"A MiG?" asked one of the British officers.

"We think there's a MiG-29 in the old hangar building at the northeast side of the airfield," explained Knowlington. His voice came over the scrambled line sharp and direct; the snap in it reminded Hack of his father. "Wong wants to have a look at it."

"Wong?" asked Preston.

"What if it takes off?" asked Hawkins.

"There is a possibility," said Wong. "A fuel truck has been positioned in the L-shaped revetment at the northernmost point of the field. The aircraft should be targeted by one of the attack planes in the support package."

"The revetment was empty yesterday afternoon, Bristol," said Hawkins. "I remember it very clearly. We were planning to use it for cover."

"Correct. As I was saying, there is a possibility the Iraqis are preparing the plane for an early morning takeoff."

"CentCom has assigned a pair of F-15's to take out the

MiG if it tries to come south," said Knowlington. "The Iraqis may have a suicide bombing run in mind. Hard to tell. In any event, if the operation against the base is going to proceed, we'd like to try and have a look at the plane before we destroy it."

"It presents a unique intelligence opportunity," added Wong.

"What does Wong know about MiGs?" said Preston.

"I know a considerable amount about Soviet weaponry," said the captain.

"You ever fly one?"

"I am not a pilot."

"We'll nail it," said Shotgun. "Maverick will slice through the hangar like a knife through a danish."

"The hell with blowing it up," said Hack. "I'll fly it out of there."

"What are you saying?" asked one of the British officers.

What was he saying? Steal it?

The idea seemed to explode in his head, and adrenaline suddenly flowed into the muscles and bones that had been worn down by the day's action.

Steal it.

"Let's fly it out," said Hack. "I can do it."

"You're out of your fucking mind," said Hawkins.

Hack jumped to his feet. "We can get it. I'll fly it. I can do it. Fuck, I know I can."

"You're going to fly a Fulcrum?" asked Shotgun.

"I already have," Preston said. "I was at Kubinka last year. Colonel, you know that. Shit. I can just walk off with it, assuming it's fueled. We can get somebody to fuel it, right? Tell them, Colonel—I was at Kubinka. I've flown MiGs."

"It's true," said Knowlington.

Kubinka was a Russian air base where Hack and three other officers had visited as part of an exchange program. Knowlington *did* know, because Preston had come back to the Pentagon directly from that assignment.

What he obviously didn't know was that Preston had flown from the backseat, doing little more than take the controls at medium altitude, and then for only a few minutes. The team's exposure to the plane had been limited and tightly controlled.

But he could do it, he knew he could do it. The idea of it—the sheer, beautiful audacity of stealing the prize right out from under Saddam's nose—he couldn't resist. No one could.

"Let's take it," he said. "I'll go in with the ground team. Bing. We're off."

"You're talking about huge risk here," said Hawkins. "Incredible risk."

"Going that far north for two SAS guys who probably aren't there isn't risky?" demanded Hack. "You're telling me that's not fucking risky?"

"I'm telling you that if there's a plane on the ground that's being refueled, we have to rethink the whole goddamn mission," said Hawkins.

"Don't chicken out on me now," said Preston.

"Screw yourself, Major."

"Okay, kids, let's all take a big breath and think about this," said Knowlington. "What if the plane is damaged, Hack? Or you can't get the fuel in it?"

"Then I jump back on the helicopter and go home. Nothing ventured, nothing gained."

"What about gear?"

"I use the Iraqis'." Hack remembered the cumbersome helmet he'd used in Russia. The flight suit, however, had been a little lighter than Western gear, and in some ways easier to use. "I take my gear as a backup, get someone to work up the connections, and hell, I just fly low and slow enough that I don't need oxygen and don't worry about pulling big-time g's. Piece of cake, Colonel."

"It's not a piece of cake," said Knowlington coldly. "Wong?"

"From an intelligence point of view," said the captain, "possession of an operational Iraqi MiG would be valuable. Very valuable. I myself would prefer acquiring it. As I began to mention to you earlier, Colonel, I considered requesting an MH-130 and a team of men to dismantle the plane at the base, returning with it."

"Very much too hazardous," said the British general in charge. "Given the proximity of other Iraqi units, no more than sixty minutes can be allotted to a ground operation."

"That's enough time."

"Potty," said another of the Brits.

"Granted, stealing the plane would require a considerable coefficient of luck," said Wong. "Nonetheless, its possession would be desirable. And the fallback situation would still result in considerable benefit; the expertise of a pilot's firsthand review of the systems would be beneficial."

"So let's get it," said Hack. He glanced at the doughnut in his hand, which he hadn't had a chance to eat. He'd squeezed it so hard that its filling had burst from the sides.

"You think the Iraqis are just going to let us take it?" said Hawkins, as sarcastic as ever.

"If Wong can get close enough to look at it, I can get close enough to steal it," said Preston, putting the doughnut down. "Let's do it."

"This isn't a game," snapped the Delta commander. "It's not rah-rah go-for-it."

Now who looked like the chickenshit?

"Major, how familiar are you with the MiG-29?" asked the British general.

"Very," said Preston, staring at the cream on his fingers. "I was on the team that reviewed the Zuyev MiG in Turkey. I flew one at Kubinka in the Soviet Union last year. It was a very limited program, General. Admittedly, I would have liked more time at the stick, but I can do this. I've flown F-15's, F-16's, and a dozen other fast-movers," he said. "I'm not just an A-10 driver. Pilot."

"Was the MiG-29 a one- or two-seater?" asked Wong.

"A two-seater," said Hack.

He glanced at Shotgun, who was not only uncharacteristically reticent, but had stopped sipping his coffee. His wingman had a frown so serious on his face that Hack looked away, focusing his attention momentarily on his cream-laden fingers. He considered licking them clean, but reached for a napkin instead.

"I saw the Zuyev plane myself," Wong said. "It does supply a baseline."

Alexander Zuyev had defected to Turkey in a Soviet MiG-29 in May 1989. His Fulcrum had been thoroughly studied; so had other examples over the past year and a half, notably those possessed by Germany and India. A great deal of intelligence had been gathered on the various export variants. But there was something about possessing an actual example—about stealing a plane from out of the pocket of the Iraqi Air Force—that was irresistible.

It was an exploit that would make anyone involved instantly famous, instantly important, even if it failed.

A quick ticket to squadron commander, and not of A-10's.

"I believe purloining the aircraft would *not* be worth the risk," said Paddington, the British intelligence expert. "A plane too far, as it were."

"Major Preston's familiarity with the aircraft would be an asset in examining it on the ground, whether we retrieved it or not," said Wong. "My expertise extends to the weapons systems only, and as he pointed out, I am not a pilot."

"If—*when* we get it," said Hack, "we'll know everything the Iraqis do."

"That would be an overstatement," said Wong.

"Kevin, what do you think?" Knowlington said, addressing the Delta Force captain.

"I think flying the plane out is a long shot, Colonel. It's a short field, and where are we going to find a mechanical crew and the helicopter to put them in?"

"We don't need a mechanical crew," said Hack. "Not if the Iraqis are already planning to fly the plane. They'll have done it all. There's auxiliary power. I go through the sequence, bring on the right engine—I can take off on one engine, start the other in the air."

"Long shot," said Hawkins.

"What's the worst-case scenario?" said Hack. "I take a look, maybe some pictures, then you blow up the plane."

"The worst-case scenario is you get killed," said Hawkins.

"I'll take the risk."

"Who's taking the risk for everyone else?"

"Our commandos must remain the priority for the mission," said the British general. "Nonetheless, I agree with Major Preston. There is a certain élan to taking the aircraft. We can supply some additional men from the squadron for the operation. We may also be able to find a mechanic with some expertise, though it is short notice." The general paused, perhaps consulting with one of his aides for a moment before returning to the line. "It is, as you say, a long shot, Captain, but one perhaps worth taking as a sidebar to the main objective."

"You sure you can get it in the air, Hack?" asked Skull. His voice sounded soft; this time it didn't remind him of his father's at all.

"Piece of cake," said Hack, as forcefully as he could. In truth, he wasn't familiar with the precise procedure for using the auxiliary power. But that was the sort of thing you could figure out on the fly.

Wasn't it?

"We'll have to replace Hack in the support package," said Skull. "That's a problem in and of itself."

Wisdom? Or folly?

More likely the latter. What if he was with the Delta team and the MiG took off before they got there? Then he'd look like a first-class boob, twiddling his thumbs on an operation that came back with *nada*. Or worse—the helicopters would be easy pickings, even for an Iraqi pilot.

Instead of being a hero, he'd look like a fool.

But you had to take risks; you had to push it. He'd been wrong to hesitate last night. He should have pushed in, not held back. War was about risks.

To steal an Iraqi plane—hell, he had to take the chance, no matter what the odds were. The payoff was just too immense, too beautiful.

Hack Preston, the man who stole Saddam's MiG. Shit, what a set of balls that guy must have.

Made general before he was thirty-five.

Chairman of the Joint Chiefs. President.

"That's not Disneyland you'd be going into," Knowlington said. "It's not Kubinka either. They're going to be shooting real bullets at you."

"If the Delta people can do it, I can," said Preston.

"Yeah, right," said Hawkins.

Hack had meant to say Captain Wong, not Delta, but for some reason the words had just come out like that. He let them stand.

"Colonel, your final assessment," the British general asked Knowlington.

Hack's doubts suddenly reasserted themselves, and he found himself wishing—wanting, hoping—that Knowlington would call it all off, say it was crazy and couldn't be done.

"If my guys think they can do it, and the D boys are up for it, then we'll take a shot," said Knowlington. "I'm going to have to hustle another pilot up to KKMC to fly Hack's plane. Lieutenant Dixon. Shotgun, you take the lead on that flight, nail the defenses the way you laid out the mission originally. I'll take the second pair and target the MiG, back you up and support the landing."

Preston looked at Shotgun across the room as the British officers began debating what additional forces could join the mission package. O'Rourke, his face as serious as a statue in the Vatican, held his hand over the mouthpiece. "You sure about this?"

"Damn sure," said Hack.

Shotgun held his stare for a long time.

"Damn sure," Hack repeated. "Damn, damn sure."

PART THREE

THIEVES

1

Skull pulled the survival vest over his flight suit. Always in the past it had felt familiar, like a well-worn coat he'd been wearing for years. But this morning it felt awkward and odd, heavier than it should, as if the pockets were filled with lead rather than a few necessities.

Knowlington double-checked his gear, moving through the preflight ritual. He'd gotten bogged down with some extraneous maintenance details and was running late, very late; Antman was buttoned up in his Hog already, waiting.

Skull was still wrestling with his decision to lead the flight. He knew he was sober, knew his fatigue and the last vestiges of his headache would clear after a breath or two of oxygen in the cockpit. He had several times the experience of anyone else he might tap to fly the mission; he could nail it with his eyes closed.

But should he go? Did he deserve to?

Wasn't a question of deserving; it was a question of duty. There was no backup—he'd sent Dixon on to KKMC already to fill in for Hack. No one else in Devil Squadron could take this gig.

So it was his duty. That was something he could handle. He took his helmet, grabbed the flight board with the map and crib notes on the mission, and began walking toward the waiting Hog.

A certain élan, the British general had said.

Damn straight. Stealing a MiG out from under Saddam's nose. What better way for a fighter jock to auger in?

Skull wasn't going to auger in. He wasn't even a fighter jock, just a Hog driver, just a washed-up commander pulling on the spurs for a last run before retirement.

Steal a MiG from under Saddam's nose? Impossible! Ridiculous!

So why had he gone along with it then?

Because he wanted to die? Because life wouldn't be worth living if he wasn't in the Air Force?

He couldn't let that be the reason. The others—his men, his people, his boys—were putting their necks on the line. They weren't doing that for some foolish, romantic notion, a vain piss in the wind that would satisfy his mistaken vanity. They were doing it to give the Allies a usable edge in the war, and maybe beyond.

How could you tell the difference? A lot of people thought that was what Vietnam was—vain, not worth the lives that were lost. He'd never believed that, though he had grieved for the friends he'd lost, the many, many people who'd died.

The war had had an effect. It had held the Soviets and the Chinese down for a while, helped divert attention from other trouble spots, in a way prevented something much, much worse.

And the truth was, sometimes you did lose, sometimes you gave it a shot and that wasn't good enough; you had to accept that and move on. This war was justified for many reasons—to calm the Middle East, to keep the balance of power, to keep oil flowing, to stop Saddam from getting the bomb. It was being run much more intelligently than Nam.

So where did this mission fit in? Two Brits who might or might not be there, a Russian-made plane that was interesting, granted, but already a known quantity, as Wong himself had admitted.

Wong. He thought it was worth it. And Wong would know. But then, he had a wild side to him beneath all his dispassionate talk about "mission coefficients" and "risk parameters." He wasn't a Pentagon desk jockey as Skull had initially thought; Wong had been involved in dozens of infiltrations and covert actions over the past few years.

The colonel walked toward his aircraft, his mind still trying to sort itself out. Maybe he wasn't up to it at all—he was experienced, yes, but he was also damn old. His reflexes and his eyes weren't what they once were. His stomach wasn't as tight, his hesitations more pronounced.

Clyston stood now at the foot of the access ladder, a stogie in his fat fist.

To say good-bye for good?

"Ready for ya, Colonel," said the sergeant.

"Let's take the walk," snapped Knowlington, already starting his preflight inspection of the plane. Fueled, armed with four AGM-65's and a pair of cluster-bombs, the Hog seethed on the apron, anxious to get going. The crew members stood a respectful distance away, craning their necks to watch as the pilot, their pilot, checked the plane, their plane.

Even though he was on a tight schedule, even though he knew an aircraft that Clyston was responsible for was an airplane so perfect it could possibly fly itself, Lieutenant Colonel Michael "Skull" Knowlington looked at the aircraft carefully and slowly. To do anything else would have seemed disrespectful to his crew. He inspected the control surfaces as if seeing them for the first time. He looked into each engine, eyeing every inch of metal. He ducked under the wings and even examined the tread on the tires. He left nothing to chance, performing the ritual as carefully as a cardinal presiding over Midnight Mass in Rome. From left to right, from front to back to front, he moved solemnly, not merely checking his plane but absorbing it, driving it deep into his being.

"Let's kick butt," he told Clyston finally.

"Don't break my plane," growled the old sergeant.

Skull chucked Clyston's shoulder—a little gentler than usual maybe, but in the same spot and with the same emotion he'd had more than twenty years before, standing beside a Thunderchief. He took a step up the ladder, then turned to give his people a well-done salute, a thank-you beyond words.

A lieutenant from the intelligence unit that shared some of Devil Squadron's HQ area came running toward the plane as he finished.

"Colonel—Colonel. General's returning your call," shouted the man, nearly out of breath. "Said he'd hold."

"Tell him you missed me," Skull shouted, climbing into the cockpit.

2

The rotor blades on the Huey bringing Dixon into KKMC couldn't quite keep up with his heart. He leaned toward the rear door of the helicopter, wind and grit whipping against his face. The roof of the large mosque across from the main area of the base gleamed with reflected light, glowing in the darkness like a candle left for an exhausted pilgrim.

Dixon steadied himself as the chopper pitched toward its landing area. He pulled the bag with his flight gear and helmet toward him, then pushed through the door as the helicopter's skids tipped down. He ran to keep his balance, adrenaline continuing to build. The smells overwhelmed him—jet fuel, diesel exhaust, burnt metal, his own sweat. Colors and dark shadows blurred around him as his eyes hunted for the vehicle that should be waiting to meet him.

"BJ! Yo, Dixon, here dude!"

Dixon turned abruptly, continuing on a dead run to a topless Humvee waiting near a building on his right.

Though the chassis of the truck was familiar, it seemed to have been modified until it looked almost like a surfer's vehicle.

"What I'm talkin' about!" shouted the driver, a large man fully dressed in flight gear—none other than Shotgun O'Rourke. "We're late. Hop in. You can chow down on the way over."

Dixon threw his gear into the rear of the special-edition Hummer and climbed aboard. It didn't surprise him that Shotgun had met him, nor was he shocked when offered a large and seemingly authentic McDonald's bag of fries and a double cheeseburger.

"My daily McDonald's fix," said Shotgun, whipping the vehicle in the direction of the life-support shop. "Figured you'd be hungry."

The food was warm—as incredible a feat, no doubt, as Shotgun's inexplicable ability to have it FedEx-ed to him in the first place. Dixon started wolfing the fries.

"Sorry. All I got's a Coke," said Shotgun, thumbing toward the back. "Was supposed to be a strawberry shake. Can't count on the help these days."

"Good to see you," said Dixon between bites.

"What I'm talking about," said Shotgun. He whipped the wheel to the right; the Hummer rose off two wheels and then plumped back down. "Got some sat pix, map for you," added the captain.

"Pictures? Of what we're hitting?"

Normally Hog drivers did without elaborate target intelligence; most guys considered getting an exact coordinate for an IP, the initial point to start an attack run, to be a comprehensive mission plan. Rarely did they work with photos of what they were going to strike.

"I take care of my guys." Shotgun whipped the wheel to the right and then back to the left, dodging a fuel truck. "We cross the border, hook up with the colonel and Antman. Go north, blah-blah-blah. Only thing we worry about is an SA-2 that has some coverage near the southwestern tip of the base. We have to jog around that, which is a pain in the butt, but once we're in it's a free ride. Not much to worry about at the target area. Right now it looks like they have two missile trucks there, SA-9's. I have 'em marked out. I take that SA-9 on the right, splash some guns on the hills overlooking the field. You get the other launcher, that gun at the far western end. Helos come in. We blow up anything that fucking moves, blah-blah-blah. Routine."

"Yup."

"Weather's improving. Shit-ass wind last night, but supposed to be calm, clear skies. Picnic weather. It's what I'm talking about."

"Uh-huh."

Shotgun turned to look at him. His voice changed, suddenly serious. "You up for this, kid?"

"You sound like my high school baseball coach."

"You up for this, kid?"

"I can nail it."

O'Rourke didn't say anything.

"I'm going to *fuck*ing nail it," Dixon said, glancing forward. "Uh, there's a truck coming."

Shotgun whipped the wheel hard, getting out of the way. His eyes remained on BJ. "Tough time up there. I heard about that little kid."

"Yeah." The word bleated from Dixon's throat, more a groan than an actual syllable with meaning.

"You got a problem, you let me know. No matter fucking what."

Dixon's mind wasn't racing or wandering and his heart didn't pound. He didn't feel nervous or antsy or overconfident or angry or anything. He just felt there, *there* in a way he hadn't been before, in a way that he couldn't process into words and wouldn't have cared to.

"Let's just kick some butt, okay?" he told Shotgun, his voice level and flat, even to his own ears.

"What I'm talking about," said Shotgun, mashing the gas pedal.

3

By the time the British transport helicopter approached the small base near the Iraqi border where the Delta and SAS team was holed up, Hack knew he was going to nail the mission. Knowlington and Wong had arranged for him to speak via satellite phone with two different Western experts on the MiG, who confirmed his own impressions and filled him with good advice. The Fulcrum was a pilot's plane, steady and predictable, faster than hell and relatively uncomplicated. It was difficult if not impossible to get her to stall or to spin unintentionally. Takeoff and landing were faster than in most Western jets, but straightforward. Piece of cake.

Of course, they didn't know the mission details, and only one of them had actually flown the plane. But that didn't matter—he was doing it.

Hack's main worry was starting the MiG off auxiliary power; he decided that if he could figure that out, he could get it into the air. The strip was very short, allegedly twelve hundred feet, which was more than four hundred less than the rated takeoff distance. But the MiG's engines were powerful as hell and the airplane had been designed for STOL or short-takeoff-and-landing operations. Hack wouldn't be carrying weapons, nor did he have to worry about having enough fuel for a round trip. Besides, the Iraqis wouldn't have landed there without having a way to get off.

Once he was in the air, it'd be a piece of cake. He would climb to thirty thousand feet and fly along a prearranged course—nearly due south, with a turn at the border. A pair of F-14's would escort him, talking to him over the UHF band. His only problem would be landing at KKMC—not technically difficult perhaps, but the first time landing an unfamiliar plane always got the adrenaline going. Still, it would be daylight, in perfect weather, with no traffic and a thousand cheerleaders.

Piece of cake.

Assuming they got the plane. The Brits had assigned forty more men to the assault team, along with a mechanic who had worked on a German MiG during a brief exchange program. But their time on the ground would be severely limited.

If the runway really was that short, maybe the Iraqis didn't actually intend on flying the plane out. The tanker truck Wong had seen might turn out to be filled with water. The MiG might turn out to have no engines or worse, much worse, just be a wooden dummy.

No way. It was his.

Returning home with a full intelligence report would be fine. Everyone at CentCom would want to talk to him. After the war it would send him on a talking tour of the Pentagon, NATO, and probably Congress as well. But he wasn't about to settle for that. He was nailing this baby, and he was going to be famous: Major Horace Gordon Preston, the man who stole Saddam's MiG.

Colonel Preston, more likely.

General Preston, without doubt.

Hack hoisted the canvas duffel bag with his backup

flight gear and jumped from the British transport helicopter as it touched down. Breaking into a trot, he ran past a set of artillery pieces sandbagged near a bunker area. The night was quiet; it was like being on a movie set, not a base a grenade's throw from the enemy.

"You're out of your fucking mind if you think we're getting that plane out of there in one piece," said Hawkins, materializing from behind a pile of sandbags. They'd never met but his voice—and attitude—were instantly recognizable. "The Iraqis aren't going to stand back and let you take it."

"Listen, Captain, you do your job, I'll do mine," Hack told him. "And I'm a major, thank you."

"That don't mean jack," said Hawkins.

By reputation as well as demeanor, Delta Force was the toughest, most daring unit in the entire U.S. military, if not the world. Hawkins pissed him off, but what did it say that he didn't think this could be done?

That Hawkins was a wimp. Because Hack was doing it.

"If you think your guys can't complete the mission, you should have said so," Preston told him.

"That's not my point," said Hawkins. His tone changed abruptly. "All right. Let me introduce you to Major Gold. He's English and he's now in charge of the assault. Wong's in with him."

Hack followed past a stack of filled sandbags and a much larger pile of unfilled ones, walking down a wide ramp bulldozed out of the desert. Hawkins disappeared around a corner; Preston found himself in a small maze, working his way through a series of Z-turns in the dark. Finally he saw a pair of guards—British SAS men, who stood as motionless as the sandbags lining the walls. Just beyond them was an open doorway, a hole in the earth filled with a faint red glow from the light within. He had to duck his head to enter; his neck muscles pulled taut, cramping with fatigue and cold.

"Major·Preston, Major Gold," said Hawkins. "You know Captain Wong."

Gold and two lieutenants were standing over a map

table a short distance away. Wong, arms crossed and face almost on the map, frowned at some of the squiggle marks on the paper. Gold extended a thin but long hand to Preston, who shook it and tried to look relaxed while the rest of the staff and some NCOs were introduced. His neck muscles had gone completely spastic, and he could feel the strain in his vertebrae.

"You'll be with my guys," Hawkins told Hack. He jabbed his finger at a corner of the table where a comprehensive diagram of the Iraqi base had been cut and pasted together from intelligence photos. A thick red marker had been used to outline buildings and other features of the base, which had been labeled "SPLASH" with capital letters above the diagram.

"We come in here, right over the runway, turn across the apron, and take a run at the MiG hangar right behind two Apaches," said Hawkins. "Depending on what we see, we land as close to the plane as we can. My guys take the hangar, move around here, secure this end of the field. Second team is going across this way, behind the hangar, cut off any approach from the highway. SAS teams should be keeping any Iraqis on the base busy. Burns has a separate team on the tanker. They come at us this way, fuel if we can."

The captain's hand flew off the diagram of the base onto a large topo map where Splash was rendered in much smaller scale.

"We'll fuel it," said Preston.

Hawkins ignored him. "There's too much resistance, we land here, beyond the approach to the runway, where we'll be covered from these guns. At that point, you and Wong wait until we secure a path to the hangar and the plane."

"If we land there," said Wong, "in effect our portion of the mission will have been called off. The timing is severe, and we should expect the Iraqis to send troops from Catin, which would be an additional risk."

Hawkins didn't contradict him. Catin was a built-up area about ten miles away. Symbols on the larger map indicated that the Iraqis had a battalion of troops and possibly helicopters based there.

"We can do it," said Preston. "Piece of cake."

"That's the spirit," said Gold. He had a singer's voice, a rich baritone that vibrated even in the cavelike bunker. "James, review the timetable, would you?"

One of the two lieutenants began running down the game plan for the assault, accenting the highlights with a flick of his hand, as if he were throwing confetti over the map. Splashdown would begin at precisely 0550, with an attack on the SA-2 site southwest of the attack area; the assault package was now so large that the planes would need to escape over the missile site's coverage area, and in any event it was past time to make sure that the site was truly dead.

Two Devil Squadron Hogs led by Shotgun would eliminate the most potent defenses at Splash itself; based on the latest intelligence, these had been expanded to include two short-range mobile missile units, more than likely SA-9's. A number of ZSU antiaircraft weapons would also be targeted; any remaining would be the first priority for the wave of Apache gunships that would spearhead the assault at 0600. Defenses neutralized, the Apaches would cover the arriving ground troops, who would strike at the buildings where the prisoners might be at precisely 0605.

Four separate groups would launch the assault. One each was devoted to the possible prisoner buildings, with a third, smaller team to be used to secure the highway leading to the base, preventing reinforcements from arriving. The fourth, made up of Delta and two different SAS squads for a total of twenty-four men, would concentrate on the hangar area and plane as Captain Hawkins had just described. Wong and Hack, along with a British mechanic with expertise on MiG systems, would fly in with Delta.

"You are to take the utmost precautions," said the lieutenant. The major nodded over his shoulder.

All told nearly one hundred and sixty men would be making the assault. Four Chinooks and a pair of American Spec Ops Blackhawk MH-60 helicopters, dubbed Pave

Hawks, had been added to the original package; there were now a total of eight transport and six attack helicopters in the plan. Two MC-130's had been added to refuel the choppers on a staggered schedule, some before the landing and some after; one of the MC-130's would double as a command plane for the major and his staff. Besides the Hogs and Tornados, four F-16's would be available to provide ground support during the latter stage of the mission. Two F-15's were watching in case the MiG managed to get off before they arrived. Four Navy F-14 Tomcats, including the pair that would trail Hack home, had been shanghaied to escort the package—a development that struck Hack as more difficult to arrange than cooperation between the Americans and Brits.

"It's a very tight schedule," said the lieutenant, summing up. He sighed contentedly, as if he had just summed up the planned menu for an elaborate meal.

"We need to be aboard the helicopters now," said Hawkins.

"Jolly good," said the British major. "Good luck to all."

Hack tried to surreptitiously unkink his neck as he followed Hawkins back out through the maze, past the artillery, and around to the helicopter landing area. The Delta force soldiers stood around their gear against some sandbags thirty yards or so from the helicopters, most of them smoking cigarettes.

"Jerry, give Major Preston the 203 and show him how to use it," Hawkins told the clump of men.

"I'd rather have an M-16," said Hack. "I'm not too bad with it."

"A 203 is an M-16 with a grenade launcher," Hawkins said, his voice so sarcastic that Hack wasn't sure he was telling the truth until the weapon was thrust into his hands. The Delta sergeant told him he wouldn't need the launcher, then demonstrated how to work it. It was a fairly straightforward device mounted below the rifle barrel; it fired 40mm grenades that looked more like fat shotgun shells than what Preston imagined a grenade to be.

"This is what they look like," the sergeant told Hack,

showing but not giving him the grenades. "One shot at a time. Give 'em loft, but not too much loft. You know what I'm saying?"

"Shit, yeah," said Hack.

The sergeant snorted. "Three hundred yards is the most they'll carry. Aim at something a hundred and fifty away, look through the quadrant—you paying attention, Major?"

"I'm all ears, Sergeant."

"You look through here, edge it up a little, just to be safe because you never done this, then push." He hit the trigger. "Make sure you got it against your shoulder snug. It ain't gonna knock you over, but you want to be more accurate than not. I'll hang on to 'em until we're on the ground. Okay?"

"Don't worry about me, Sergeant. I know what I'm doing."

"You use an M-16 before?"

"I have a marksman badge," snapped Preston.

The sergeant smiled as if to say, "Ain't that sweet."

"Excuse me, Major," said Wong, "but I wanted to review our priorities before we start."

"Flight gear is number one," said Preston. "There must be some sort of life-support shop near the plane. I think the hangar, but maybe with the fuel truck or in that area. I want to talk with the men who—"

"Our priority is to survey the airplane. I am primarily interested in the avionics," said Wong. "And any missiles. You should concentrate on any upgrades to the control system inside the cockpit. Our British sergeant will examine the fuel capacity and engine. The type is regularly detuned to extend maintenance intervals, which naturally affects its performance. After that, he will survey the flight control surfaces. The flaps—"

"I need the gear to fly," Hack told him. "My connectors are kludges, and even if they work I won't have a radio."

"Taking the plane is secondary to our main objective of intelligence gathering."

Hack curled the rifle beneath his arm. He'd blast his

way into the stinking hangar single-handedly if he had to. Screw Wong and the Delta jerks.

A flak vest hit him in the side, nearly knocking him down.

"Gear up," said Fernandez. "Both of ya. You're gonna wanna pee before you get on the helicopter. Otherwise you're pissin' out the door, which means into the wind, which usually means in your face." He snickered. "No sense wettin' your pants till the fun starts."

4

Shotgun did a quick check of his instruments, then reached down to his Twizzlers pocket for a fresh supply of licorice. He and Dixon were running a good ten minutes ahead of schedule, and in fact a simple flick of the wrist would put him practically on the planned IP or ingress point to start the attack. Ten seconds beyond that he'd be able to cursor in his first SAM and reach for a celebratory Three Musketeers bar.

In just about any other line of work, running ahead of schedule was a good thing. But here being ten minutes early was nearly as bad as being ten minutes late. Striking now might cost the assault teams the advantage of surprise they were counting on. Worse, the ten minutes they had to wait was potentially ten minutes' worth of fuel they wouldn't have to support the commandos and Delta boys when the fun started.

At least his stock of candy was strong. He had two more packs of Twizzlers, a full complement of Tootsie Rolls,

three bags of M&M's, and four oversized Three Musketeers bars in his specially designed candy pockets. And that
didn't count the pastry in his vest, nor the backup Pepper-
mint Patties and the gumdrops taped under the dash. Of
course, if things got really desperate, Shotgun could always dig into the survival stash attached to the seat. But
you didn't want to get into your contingencies if you could
help it.

"Yo, Devil Two, we're spinning this orbit another few
minutes. Splash is on time," he assured his wingman.

"Two," acknowledged Dixon.

The sharp click reminded O'Rourke of Doberman, very
businesslike as tee time approached. Dixon had some of
the Dogman's moves as well, and while he wasn't yet the
marksman Glenon was, he still had acquitted himself well
enough to nail an Iraqi helicopter with his cannon during
the early hours of the air war. Of course, no one had
Doberman's explosive temper, but that wasn't necessarily
a bad thing. BJ was a kick-ass Hog driver; Shotgun's six
would be well covered when they made the attack.

Still, O'Rourke felt slightly unsettled—not uneasy and
certainly not worried, just slightly out of whack. The thing
was, he wasn't used to playing lead guitar. He was more
like Miami Steve, humping in the background. Oh, yeah,
doing very important work, but not actually fronting the
band. Hitting the notes, setting the rhythm, working the
solos even—but not *the Boss*. Playing lead had a different
head to it.

Splash had grown so complicated that it was now being
coordinated by its own control plane, code-named Head
but mostly referred to as Splash Control by the others in
the package—another little thing that p'd Shotgun off,
because what was the sense of having a call sign if you
weren't going to use the thing. Head came over the circuit,
counting down the time to Splashdown—thirty minutes
away.

"Devil One acknowledges, Headman," said Shotgun.
"On station."

On station. *On station.* If he were the wingman, he

could have said something like "Got your butts covered," or "Cheery-oh" and asked after the Queen. Because a wingman could do that kind of thing.

Flying lead, you had to be serious.

No wonder Doberman was such a grouch.

The Tornado tagged with nailing the SA-2 radar site southwest of the target area checked in. They were running five minutes late. So were the Splash Apaches, which according to the support craft had had trouble refueling. The helicopters themselves did not actually come on the circuit; given that they were much more vulnerable to the Iraqi defenses, they were on radio silence until the attack began. Besides, they were flying so low—roughly six feet above the desert floor—that it would have been difficult for the command ship to communicate with them directly.

Six feet above ground level. That was where Shotgun's Hog wanted to be. She was getting a nosebleed up here at eighteen thousand. Other planes flew such altitudes routinely; most might even consider it low in a war zone. But an A-10 pilot this high looked around for asteroids to avoid.

Shotgun's A-10 grumbled as they took a bank to avoid the outer reaches of the SA-2's radar. He patted the throttle, trying to soothe her.

"I'll take you down soon," he said. "I promise. Think of it this way—the higher we are, the faster we dive."

Unimpressed, the A-10 continued to stutter. It was subtle perhaps, but it was definitely coughing when it had no reason to cough.

Shotgun glanced at the instruments—the temp was rising on engine two. His oil pressure was good, but there was something wrong with the power plant, whose rpms were fluctuating. He throttled back gently, lightly trimming the rest of the plane to compensate.

The temp edged higher. Then the oil pressure began whipping up and down, with the turbine's rpms doing the same.

A wingman with a full complement of bombs and Twinkies could have ignored the readings as either a product of misplaced sensitivity on the gauges' part, or his own overworked imagination. But a pilot leading an important element of the attack had to assess them coolly and coldly and conclude that, against all odds, against all human experience, one of the A-10A's engines was actually threatening to quit.

Couldn't be happening. Shotgun chewed his Twizzlers contemplatively, adjusting the rest of the aircraft's systems to compensate.

The engine sputtered.

"Shape up," he told his plane, smacking the fuel panel switches as if the problem were due to indigestion.

The Hog responded by surging nearly sideways, the engine suddenly back in the green, all indicators at spec. Then Shotgun heard a soft pop behind him and felt a shudder; by the time the warning lights told him the engine had put in for early retirement, he was muscling the stick to keep the heavily laden plane from spinning toward the ground.

5

Skull moved his eyes carefully, using them as an as-
tronomer might use a telescope to examine an uncharted
planet. Nudging them across the reddish-blue band of the
horizon, he studied the thin wisps of clouds for black
specks and odd shifts, looking for enemy fighters that
might somehow have managed to avoid the comprehensive Allied radar net.

That was virtually impossible for a primitive air force like
the Iraqis'. But Knowlington had learned to fly against a supposedly primitive air force. The Vietnamese MiGs were out-
dated, outmoded, and son-of-a-bitchin' good. They came at
you from a cloud or caught your tail or suckered you into a
turn where their wingman popped up behind you. They hid
in the sun, or the blind spot of your inattention. They waited
until you were out of missiles, or low on fuel. They took advantage of your arrogance and sloppiness, your failure to hit
the marks with precision. It was more the men than the ma-
chines—but that had always been the case, back to the very

beginning over the trenches in France and Belgium. Skill and machine and luck.

Never forget luck, the underrated factor in every equation.

Skull's eyes reached the right wing of his Hog, then slipped upward, the ritual search beginning again. He blew a long breath into his mask, nudged his stick just barely left, staying on course. A hundred other missions played at the edge of his brain, memories of mistakes and triumphs that pricked up his adrenaline. A list of contingent to-do's played constantly at the back of his head: if this, then that; if that, then this. Skull had only the vaguest awareness of the list, knew only that if it was needed his brain would flash it like an urgent bulletin to his arms and legs and eyes. His actions would be automatic.

To fly, you had to think and not think at the same time. To fly well, you had to forget you were flying and pretend you weren't thinking.

An old instructor had told him that. Skull could still remember nodding solemnly at the time, not knowing what the hell the geezer was talking about. Knowlington had shot down two Vietnamese MiGs before he started to actually understand—before, really, the tension of combat became familiar enough to relax him. Before the jagged rhythm of an overpumped heart became a thing to live for.

He was giving that up. It was his duty to resign.

Who wanted to go out that way, sneaking off in the middle of the night? Better to burn out in a last fireball.

That was why he'd gone along with the plan to steal the MiG. One last burst of glory. He wasn't coming back from this mission. Auger in.

Years from now, people would talk about him in awed tones: Michael Knowlington, the guy who bought it carrying out the impossible dream.

Arrogance. Vanity.

He tightened his eyes and continued scanning the sky.

6

Shotgun wrenched the stick right, crunching the rudder pedals at the same time, more for leverage than actual effect. The plane's wings finally steadied and he started working his nose back up, regaining control. He'd lost nearly three thousand feet in little more than the time it took to chew through a half-stick of red licorice.

That was nothing. He'd dropped the other half of the candy, losing it somewhere on the floor of the plane. That was the kind of thing that hurt your ego, as well as attracted ants.

Cycling through the restart procedure on the starboard engine, he considered that what he really needed right now was a good cup of Joe, something beyond the Dunky in his thermos. Dunkin' Donuts made a mean batch of caffeine, but in a situation like this there was no beating the takeout at Joltin' Joe's Diner in Schenectady, N.Y. Shotgun had thought several times of arranging a pipeline for just such emergencies, but hadn't been able to come up with a way of keeping the coffee hot in transport to the Gulf. A cold jolt didn't do it.

At the moment, he'd take any jolt, cold or hot. The power plant just wasn't willing to restart, and nothing he did—including a very unsubtle string of curses and a harsh rap on the instrument panel—worked.

"Hey, Two! Yo, kid, I got a situation up here," he told Dixon. "One of my motors thinks it belongs in a Ford."

"One?"

"Left engine died."

Shotgun checked his position against the paper map on his knee board as Dixon acknowledged. He'd drifted west, edging dangerously close to the SA-2 site, which wasn't due to be taken out for a good ten minutes. So close, in fact, that a direct course to his target area would take him inside the targeting envelope.

"Here's what I'm thinking," he told his wingman. "We change the game plan slightly—I'll go after the SA-9's, then nail the guns with the cluster-bombs."

"Uh, lost some of that, One," said Dixon. "You're looking to hit all the targets on one engine?"

"What I'm talking about," said Shotgun. "Can't fly with all this weight under my wings. Might as well get rid of it where it'll do the most good."

"Uh, Captain—" Static swallowed the rest of Dixon's voice. His meaning, however, was clear. Shotgun was out of his mind to not cut his stores loose and head home.

Maybe if he'd been flying another plane, that might have been true. But in a Hog, Shotgun's decision made perfect, logical, conservative sense. At least to him.

"Got to shoot my wad," explained O'Rourke. "This way, I get rid of it quick and leave you a full load to back up the assault team with. Let me get what we know is there; you handle the contingencies. I'll turn around as soon as I'm out of arrows, I promise. You hang with Splash."

"You're flying back alone?"

"I think I take a left and keep going until the stop sign, right?" Shotgun lifted his finger off the mike, remembering he was the flight leader and had to make a pass at sounding like one.

What would Doberman do in this situation?

Curse and snarl something nasty.

Couldn't curse the kid, though. It was tough to be nasty to BJ.

"Unless you're thinking of pushing, it's not going to make much difference you're on my butt or not going home," said Shotgun. "Besides, I don't want you to miss the show."

Under duress, Shotgun might have admitted that he knew vaguely of some sort of standing order or suggestion or maybe whimsical thought somewhere about how to deal with engine failures that might, under certain very specific circumstances, be interpreted as advising against proceeding to a target on one engine. He'd also admit, again under heavy duress, that though the plane could fly quite adequately with one engine once properly coaxed and flattered, she wasn't particularly happy to do so while carrying a full load—a fact she emphasized now by giving him a stall warning.

He traded a little altitude for speed. Time to go for it.

"You with me, Two?"

"Your call, Gun."

"What I'm talking about. One other thing," he added. "I want you to leave me and track back to our original course. I have to cut a closer line to Splashdown."

"Uh—" The rest of his transmission was covered with static.

"You got to work on that stutter, kid," said Shotgun. "Mars a really beautiful singing voice."

"Anything like a straight line is going to take you through the target area for the SA-2."

"Our British buddies are going to take it out any second," said Shotgun.

There was a pause. O'Rourke knew what Dixon was going to say. It was, after all, exactly what he would say.

"I got your butt," said Dixon.

"Kid—"

"You really ought to think about upgrading your choice of toilet paper," said his wingman. "And maybe doing something about that hair."

"What I'm talking about," said Shotgun, nosing onto the course.

7

BJ kept his eyes nailed on Shotgun's good engine. He'd always thought O'Rourke was a little crazy, but this was insane. In approximately ten seconds they were going to cross into the scanning area of one of the most potent missiles in the Iraqi arsenal, a missile that had been downing Western aircraft for something like thirty years. If the SAM operators decided to target the A-10's—and even if no radar anywhere in Iraq had detected them, the planes were certainly low and slow enough to have been eyeballed by now in the early light—the chugging Hog was dead meat.

Insisting that he take all the targets was equally insane. The Maverick launches were one thing—the AGM-65's could be targeted and fired from a good distance away. But the cluster-bombs had to be released essentially over the target, which meant that likely as not O'Rourke would be plunging into a hail of flak to kick them off. With one engine—hell, with two—yanking and banking to duck even optically guided 23mm shells was not an easy way to make a living. Half the push as you recovered meant the gunners had twice the chance to nail you.

BJ shifted against his seat restraints, hunkering over his stick, pushing himself into the SA-2's red zone.

The Iraqi missile was probably dead. It hadn't come up last night. Wouldn't now.

Dixon checked his weapons panel, made sure he was ready to go with the Mavs, glanced at the targeting screen. It took patience to work the blurs into a hittable target, and he wasn't feeling particularly patient.

His mind flashed on Becky, the warm feel of her body next to his in bed, her softness.

He wanted her warmth. He hadn't realized how good it could feel before, or perhaps he hadn't needed it before. It didn't erase everything, it didn't banish the memory of the kid or everything else, but it was something he wanted. He didn't feel cold anymore.

BJ's eyes itched. He moved them up from the screen, looked outside the plane, checked the HUD, went back to the IR image in the video.

The target area dribbled into the top corner of the screen. Dixon found the dim shadow of an SA-9 launcher, or at least thought he did—definitely yes. He slipped the cursor toward it in case Shotgun missed. He took a breath and checked his altitude, nudging below thirteen thousand feet. His left hand tightened on the throttle and he looked toward Shotgun's plane, watching for the burst that would show he'd fired, waiting for the yell in his ears over the short-range radio announcing the game was on.

He waited, but what he heard was not Shotgun's triumphant screech but the warning blare of the RWR and a scream from the AWACS controller, their impromptu duet announcing that the Iraqi SA-2 battery had launched a pair of missiles in their direction.

8

Captain Hawkins leaned forward, trying to see their target area through the Pave Hawk's windscreen. It would have taken better eyes than he possessed—Splash was still a good ten miles away. The two helo pilots worked silently in the cockpit, fingers jumping across the cockpit panels in an elaborate ballet. Every so often one would point to something; inevitably the gesture would be answered by a thumbs-up.

The aircraft the two men were flying was based on the Sikorksy S-70/H-60 Blackhawk, the military's standard utility helicopter. The successor to the ubiquitous UH-1 Huey, the base model could carry an eleven-man squad and three or four crew members roughly six hundred miles before refueling. While combat use generally shortened the range, the type was considerably faster and longer-legged than the versatile Huey. The MH-60G Pave Hawk—an Air Force ship often used on Spec Ops missions, as well as for combat SAR or rescue operations—

differed from the standard H-60 in several key aspects. Among the most important for this mission were advanced ground-following radar, an infrared radar, satellite communications and position finder, and range-extending fuel tanks.

Hawkins pushed back against the wall of the helicopter, tightening his grip on the restraining strap. He'd been standing pretty much the whole way. He hated sitting for more than five minutes as a general rule, and going into combat he could never sit, could hardly even stand still. He didn't fidget over the operational details, much less worry about what might go wrong or what could go wrong. He didn't check his gear a million times; once after takeoff was good enough for him. But he couldn't sit, and he couldn't stand still.

Most of the D boys were standing too. The exception was Fernandez, whom he'd told to mind Major Preston and the British mechanic, who were crouched on the floor talking about the MiG. The Delta sergeant perched on a jumpseat behind the two men, occasionally glaring at their backs like an angry baby-sitter.

The British mechanic was an older man who looked as if he'd been rousted from bed. Huddled beneath an oversized parka, he looked more like a mound than a man, his limbs hunched together, his face whiter than porcelain. The man had no more volunteered for this mission than Fernandez had asked to watch him; how much he might really be able to accomplish was anyone's guess, even though he did seem to know a lot about the plane. He'd told Hawkins his name was Eugene, pronouncing it with great emphasis on both syllables. If he had a last name, it had been drowned out by the noise of the helicopter.

Preston kept gesturing and nodding. Obviously a blowhard, the Air Force major had no perspective on anything beyond his nose.

What the hell did *any* pilot know about war anyway? The fucks flew a million miles away from any real danger. They popped up, pushed a button, went home. That was their war—roll around with a local girl, try to forget the hardship involved in drinking beer instead of champagne.

Granted, some of the A-10 pilots were different. The guys flying in the support package especially.

Doberman had personally saved Hawkins's butt by nailing a MiG in air-to-air combat. He was a nasty son of a bitch with a temper so fierce he would have been washed out of Special Operations training—hell, out of the Army—in maybe five minutes. But he used it to his advantage in the air.

BJ Dixon had humped a rucksack and saved one of Hawkins's best squad leaders. To hear the old coot talk about the pilot now, you'd think he was in love. Dixon had lived off the land for a couple of days and managed to get his butt snared in a STAR pickup—so you knew he wasn't the usual wimpshit pilot.

Shotgun—what a piece of work. Stranded temporarily at Fort Apache, he'd helped one of Hawkins's sergeants capture a tanker truck that turned out to be a chemical weapons ferry. Even more impressive, the SOB had won a desert "dune buggy" off a Spec Ops command in a poker game and knew more about weapons than half the guys in Delta Force.

And Colonel Knowlington had bona fides that stretched back from before Hawkins was born. So four exceptions to the general rule of pilots being shitheads.

The only other Air Force officer that Hawkins knew well was Bristol Wong, and Wong was in a whole different category—Wong was a Spec Ops guy born and bred, assigned to the Air Force by some weird fit of fate, or maybe as penance for serious sins in an earlier lifetime. Just now he was leaning over the door gunner, no doubt offering some arcane tip on how to increase the weapon's accuracy.

But Preston was a typical goober. No way was he getting the plane out.

Hawkins suspected the MiG would be gone before they got there. The Iraqis weren't quite as dumb as they seemed.

But what the hell. They were in it now.

He turned his head and glanced toward the sliding window, where one of the crewmen was fingering the 7.62mm mini-gun. A long tube attached to the gun would catch spent shells, ferrying them outside where they could be safely ejected. The gun was similar to the SAW Hawkins had outfitted himself with, and nicely supplemented the .50-cal door-mounted weapon.

Zipping over Iraqi territory at more than a hundred miles an hour, their route had been carefully planned to follow an empty path in the desert; they had seen no sign of life except for two highways in the last half hour. Now, as he looked past the gunner, Hawkins saw, or thought he saw, a row of houses only a few yards away. He pushed forward, trying to get a better view, not sure if the Iraqi village was an optical illusion or a detail he had somehow missed when the pilots went over the ingress route with him.

Illusion—just rocks. Or rather hills.

But there were buildings there, a half mile away, no more. People or animals or something moving, something live.

The sky flashed red in the distance. One of the crew members began talking loudly, relaying radio information from the command plane.

The chopper seemed to pick herself up by the tail, her pace quickening. The door gunner leapt forward to man his weapon.

"Missiles in the air ahead! Flak!" warned the copilot. "The game's afoot!"

A Sherlock Holmes fan, thought Hawkins, glancing at his watch. They were five minutes from Splashdown.

9

Shotgun nailed the cursor on the SA-9 just as the missile warning blared. The timing couldn't be more perfect—his CD player had just dished up "Rock the Casbah" by the Clash.

"Sing it, boys," he told the band, joining in on the chorus as he goosed the first missile toward the small mobile launcher, which was just over eight nautical miles away. A second, unbriefed launcher sat maybe twenty yards to the right of the first; Shotgun zeroed the targeting pipper on the hatch right in front of the four-barreled launching arm and cooked off Maverick number two.

He kicked chaff out, but didn't bother zagging to avoid the SA-2—the way he figured it, he was flying so damn slow, a cut left or right wasn't going to throw the enemy missile anyway. Besides, it would make it even harder to find the other SA-9 launcher, which didn't seem to be in the shadows of the hill where it was supposed to be. Perhaps sensing his difficulty, the Iraqis kindly lit their ZSU-

23 flak guns, streaming bullets into the sky to advertise his secondary targets.

"I'll get to you, I'll get to you," he told them, realizing from the position of the ZSU-23's that he had been looking for the other SA-9 a little too far to the east. He slipped his cursor left, working the gear like his grandpa used to nudge the old Philco to improve reception. "Light touch, young'un, that's what it takes," Grandpa O'Rourke always used to advise, and just like that the baseball game would flood in.

"There it goes!" shouted Phil Rizzuto, the Yankee Scooter calling a Roy White home run into the upper deck in right field. The Maverick target cue nudged into the sloped grille of the SA-9 Gaskin launcher, itself a throwback to the days of stifled offense and a big strike zone. The Russian-made launcher lacked White's deceptive speed, and couldn't play the difficult sun of Yankee Stadium's left field, but it did possess something of the outfielder's quiet grit—the launcher puffed up two missiles just as Shotgun sent his fastball its way.

"Nice try, my friends," Shotgun told the Iraqis. He was just coming into the missiles' extreme range. Essentially hopped-up SA-7 heat-seekers on a mobile platform, the Gaskins had limited intelligence and were relatively small, though of course any amount of explosive with wings attached was nothing to sneeze at. Shotgun kicked defensive flares and deepened his angle of attack, sliding right as he came for the AAA guns at the foot of the hill to the right of the airstrip. He found four of them, staggered in pairs, each pumping enough lead in the sky to keep a million batteries from ever running out of juice. Shotgun thumbed his last Maverick at the first stream he could designate, then pushed his Hog right, leaning against his good engine to get an acceptable glide path for his CBUs.

Problem was, the bombs were preset for release around five thousand feet, and there was no way he was going to be that high when he got over the target. He couldn't fudge it either—he was passing through seven thousand already and very far off the mark.

The air percolated with exploding shells, the gunners homing in on the chugging target. Shotgun wasn't quite in their range, though that didn't stop them from giving it the ol' Iraqi college try.

Nor did it prevent at least a few shells from bursting close enough to the Hog's skin to rattle the wings.

"Gonna melt your barrels you keep shooting like that," he told them.

People were yelling at him over the radio. The Clash had moved on to "Red Angel Dragnet." The Hog added a few jangles and rumbles of its own. The SA-2 plowed through the air somewhere behind him. The SA-9's sped upward somewhere to the left. The 23mm slugs angled for his nose. Shotgun felt right at home.

Almost perfect.

"I could really go for a good cup of Joe right now," he told the Iraqis, pushing his nose down sharply. "Got any?"

His Maverick erupted, erasing the first Zeus.

"I'll take that as a no," he said, dropping his bombs into the flak dealer to its right. The Hog jerked slightly as the bombs fell, helping as Shotgun pushed right for the second group of guns, which inexplicably stopped firing before he pickled.

"I told you not to start firing too soon," Shotgun told the Iraqis as he pulled back on the stick. "Damn. Didn't the Russkies teach you anything?"

"One, repeat?"

"Oops, did I transmit there?" Shotgun asked Dixon over the squadron frequency.

"You've been doing play-by-play," answered his wing-man.

"Any good?"

"Don't give up your day job. That the Clash on the sound track?"

"What I'm talking about," said Shotgun, who always appreciated when a youngster picked up on the classics. He checked his position—three thousand feet, give or take, a mile north of Splashdown, airspeed 185 knots.

Must have a tailwind, he thought.

"Yo, kid, what happened to that SA-2?"

"Got confused and blew up right after launch," BJ told him. "Tornados nailed the site right after the radar came on. Gave them a good beacon."

"Always glad to help out our allies, even if I'm just playing clay pigeon." Shotgun flicked the CD player back to the beginning of disc one; something about "Know Your Rights" always got his juices moving.

"Gun, did you hear me warn you about that SA-9 launch?"

"Musta missed it," Shotgun told him. A gun far to the north began firing, probably at him. The defenses to the north and west were serious and numerous; he banked southward, still climbing slowly. He could just make out Dixon beyond the thick gray smoke rising from his targets. "You got it, kid?"

"I'm taking a run at the field now," Dixon told him.

"Go for it," said Shotgun. He checked his instruments, working through the numbers more slowly than usual—a difference of approximately one nanosecond.

Fuel a little lighter than he'd expected. More than enough to make it back to KKMC, though, especially on one engine. Shit, it was all pretty much downhill from here.

Shotgun spotted Dixon's Hog diving toward the smoking airfield. A plume of black smoke erupted in its path; the dark fingers climbed high into the air, far higher than the ZSU-23 had been.

"Heavy artillery gunnin' for ya, kid," Shotgun shouted as Dixon's plane disappeared in the geyser of 57mm shells.

10

Dixon hadn't seen the antiaircraft gun in the web of shadows and smoke. The first shells—fat twists of glowing metal hurling past his windscreen—seemed unreal, old nightmares remembered long after sleep.

If he'd seen it, he could have nailed the obsolete but still deadly self-propelled ZSU-57-2 gun with his AGMs, dropped the CBUs, or even lit his cannon and erased it with a quick burst of combat load. But Dixon wasn't seeing very well—or rather, he was seeing in slow motion. It had been less than two weeks since he'd last flown, but those two weeks had been a lifetime. Shapes that would have crystallized immediately into threats remained vague and distorted for an agonizingly long time before he deciphered them.

In truth, the difference might have only been a matter of a few seconds, but in war, under fire, a few seconds was the difference between life and death. He pushed his Hog right, ducking the path of the flak, increasing his speed as he dove.

The gun firing at him threw massive shells to twelve thousand feet in the air, but it was an ancient system, manually aimed. The bullets chewed the air behind the Hog, not quite fast enough to catch the plane's tail.

Gravity smashed into Dixon's head as he zagged away. Weighed down by her munitions, trying to respond to her pilot's harsh inputs, the plane slammed downward. The flight suit tried desperately to compensate for the forces trying to squeeze blood from BJ's body, but there was only so much it could do. Dixon felt his head begin to float above his body, icy blackness poking at the edges of his consciousness.

This had happened to him before.

On his very first combat mission, a fistful of negative g's had shaken him so badly he'd launched his weapons without targets, broken his attack, run away.

He didn't do that now. If the days that had passed since he last flew had robbed him of his instantaneous reactions, they had also changed him irrevocably. He might flinch, but he would never run away from anything ever again. He would bite his teeth together hard enough to taste blood flowing from the gums, hard enough to taste the smoking cordite of the grenade that had killed the boy, hard enough to hold off the yawning blackness of fear. And then he would do his job, without fail.

As the g's backed off, Dixon pushed the Hog into a wide banking turn, his hand reaching to the armament panel. Close on the target, below the prime altitude for dropping the cluster-bombs, he selected his cannon. He straightened his wings, saw the thick line of flak turning toward him, and pushed the trigger. The seven-barreled Gatling spun in the Hog's chin, spitting spent uranium into the open gondola of the Iraqi gun. Metal hissed into steam, and another vehicle parked near the 57 erupted in a fireball as Dixon's bullets caught it. He let go of the trigger, quickly scanning the area for another target. There were dug-in positions on the hills opposite the airstrip; small weapons, probably, nothing that could hurt him, but a problem for the assault teams.

No other defenses. And damn—there was the MiG, sitting near the hangar just waiting for Preston to come and snatch her.

"Kid! Kid!" screamed Shotgun.

"I'm here. Nailed the gun," said Dixon.

"Yeah, I see that," said O'Rourke.

"Climbing," BJ told him, double-checking the ladder on his HUD as he cleared five thousand feet. "Going to take out some trenches on those hills with the CBUs, then clear Splash in."

"What I'm talkin' about."

The enemy positions on the hill looked like a series of thumbprints on a misshapen cookie. BJ rolled on them, descending quickly into the sweet spot of his bomb swoop and pickling right on target. The Mk 20 Rockeye II Mod. 2's were veritable bomb dump trucks. Their munitions fanned out in an elaborate and deadly pattern as the CBU unit ignited over its target. The bombs were capable of piercing light armor, and could do very nasty things to flesh.

Dixon recovered, sweeping his eyes around the battlefield one last time.

"Splash zone is clear," he announced, glancing at his watch. They were two minutes ahead of schedule.

11

The helicopter's tail whipped so hard to the left that Hawkins fell sideways, losing his balance as the door gunner began blasting away at a defensive post near the southern end of the runway. One of the Apaches roared across their path, bullets whipping from its chain gun. Hawkins pushed upright and caught sight of the MiG, sitting in front of the hangar not ten yards away. The Pave Hawk veered back right, whipping around—one, maybe two Iraqis were running from the plane back toward the hangar, cement flying around them as the door gunner and the Minigun operator turned their attention on them.

The plane was out in the open, canopy up, a ladder nearby. The hangar door was open. Another Apache crossed between the plane and the building, unmolested.

The ragheads had been caught completely by surprise. Idiots!

You couldn't pray for luck like this.

"Down! Down!" Hawkins yelled, anxious to get on the

ground. "Get us on the runway! In front of the plane! In front of the plane!"

The Pave Hawk had already pitched toward the ground, fluttering and then coasting as if on a gentle wave. It touched down not five yards from the nose of the enemy plane. Crowley leapt through the open door. Pig followed, with Wong right behind him. "Go! Go! Go!" Hawkins yelled to the others, leaping forward himself. Only Fernandez, with Preston and Eugene, remained behind.

The helicopter jerked forward as Hawkins went out. He tripped against the edge of the doorway, but somehow managed to keep his feet squared so that he hit the cement clean, even though he was falling off balance. He rolled, got up, whipped the nose of his heavy gun around to cover the MiG. Satisfied that the plane was empty, he ran toward the hangar. He caught sight of the British Chinook with its SAS team descending beyond the northeastern corner of the hangar area. The commandos were uncharacteristically late, though only by a few seconds—their big helo had dropped nearly straight down, obviously not encountering any resistance.

We're in, we're in, he thought. Wong and that bozo Preston are going to pull it off.

Hot shit.

Hangar. Stop celebrating and secure the hangar.

Hawkins pushed forward, spotting Crowley at the large open door. The sergeant reached his hand back and Hawkins threw himself down, realizing his point man was going to toss a flash-bang into the building, neutralizing any resistance with a grenade.

It wasn't necessarily the optimum move—there were maybe a dozen flammable substances inside a typical hangar that the grenade could easily ignite. A fire could ruin the plane, not to mention snare Crowley. But in the fury of the moment he wasn't thinking about that.

The grenade went off. He pumped another. There was a puff of smoke, but no secondaries. The Iraqis who had run for the hangar were either dead or severely wounded.

Something flashed from the hedge of dirt on Hawkins's

right. He whirled around, saw Pig near the crest of the berm working his MP5.

"Secure the plane! Secure the plane!" Hawkins yelled before realizing that Wong was already doing just that—and in fact had started to wheel the large, unpowered ladder platform toward the cockpit.

Hawkins had turned back toward the helo to look for Fernandez when a tan stick popped up in his peripheral vision from near the hangar. Hawkins jerked around, pressing his trigger at the same time. His SAW cut the Iraqi in half.

The captain dropped to one knee, covering the area more carefully; when he was satisfied that there were no other soldiers there, he jumped up and ran toward the ditch the Iraqi had hid in, quickly making sure no one was hiding beyond the hangar.

The trench ran down from the helicopter through a small sewer pipe at the edge of the berm. A thick black gook covered the bottom. The image of oil draining from an old car engine clogged his mind.

A jet roared overhead and two Chinooks stuttered in on his left, the reserves being ordered in to help one of the units. Dirt flew into his face. "Incoming! Incoming!" yelled someone.

The damn A-10 is firing at us, Hawkins thought.

Then a fresh spray of dirt and chips of cement showered over his head, and he realized that the Iraqis were firing some sort of mortar from beyond the hump of dirt below the hangar and runway area.

"Incoming!" yelled someone, and Hawkins realized it was him. Something ripped over his head, a hot stream of air pushing him flat on the cement apron in front of the MiG—the Pave Hawk had jerked upward, giving the machine gunners an angle on the mortar.

Crowley had raced to the far end of the berm beyond the hangar, pumping his 203. Crowley's grenade and the Pave Hawk's machine-gun bullets hit the Iraqi defenders at the same time. Blood and dirt flared into a large secondary explosion behind them. A vehicle had been wedged into the berm, and Crowley's grenade ignited the gas tank.

They had the bastards nailed now.

"Let's go! Let's go!" Hawkins shouted. He turned around, saw that Wong was on the plane. One of his men was following up the berm.

Secure against counterattack.

Crowley and Pig were already blazing away at two knots of Iraqis in ditches nearly a hundred yards away. Those trenches had obviously been intended as fallback positions for attacks from the south, and were open to the berm. The only retreat was across an open road, with another hundred to two hundred yards to the nearest shelter, a small wall in front of a set of two or three small bunkers or perhaps bomb shelters. Hawkins's men had the Iraqis in them pinned down, though they didn't have enough of an angle to get them all.

Two Apaches were concentrating on a vehicle or a bunker or something about three hundred yards to his right, across and well beyond the runway. The rest were whipping back and forth above the two barracks-type buildings the SAS guys were attacking. Heavy machine-gun fire announced that the Iraqis were putting up stiff resistance. Smoke poured from one of the windows.

He turned and called for Krushev, his com specialist. The team tasked with grabbing the fuel truck had landed; its Chinook was still on the ground. He couldn't tell whether they had met resistance or not.

Wong was lying across the wing of the MiG.

Hit?

Hit?

No. The intel expert jumped up and then did a hand-roll off the wing, obviously inspecting something.

So where the fuck was Preston? Had the prissy major wimped out under fire?

12

Hack slammed his knee against the helicopter door. His body slid sideways into the open air, the world pirouetting around in a grayish-white tangle. His head slammed hard against the concrete and he cursed, his lungs flaming with anger as he pushed back to his feet, then collapsed, his knee crumbling with pain.

Smoke and the spent exhaust of the helicopter hung thick in the air, making it difficult to breathe and even harder to think. An Apache gunship whipped toward him, its nose gun revolving downward as if Preston were being targeted. Something tried pushing him down from behind; Hack wheeled around and slammed the butt end of the M-16 at it, only to realize that it was Fernandez, the Delta sergeant assigned to get him safely off the helicopter. The blow landed against Fernandez's side, but if he felt it the sergeant gave no hint. The burly Delta trooper set Preston on his feet, then ran back to the helicopter to get Eugene, the British mechanic.

A ladder had been pushed near the plane. Hack hobbled, then skipped, finally gaining momentum and managing a full run. But before he could get to the ladder the ground rocked with a heavy explosion. He lost his balance and dropped his rifle as he spun. Once more he slammed his head hard against the concrete of the runway access apron as he landed.

Something red covered his eyes—he thought the MiG had exploded, felt a pit in his stomach, anger as his opportunity, his once-in-a-lifetime opportunity, ebbed from him. Cursing, he got to his feet, so mad that he nearly smashed the rifle barrel end into the ground. He might have tried putting the fire out with his bare hands, but with his first step he realized the MiG hadn't exploded. It stood not five feet away, untouched by the chaos around it.

"Major, I am ready for your assessment," said Wong, his voice calm as he appeared at Preston's side. He nudged Preston toward the other side of the plane, where a large boarding ladder constructed of tubular steel sat next to the cockpit. Painted bright orange, the contraption looked like a piece of scaffolding for a construction site.

It held Preston's weight easily. With his rifle in one hand, he climbed up quickly and touched the cobra cowling along the forward fuselage. The fin extended from the wing and helped give the Russian plane extraordinary flight stability in difficult maneuvers.

The cold metal stung his bare hand. Hack ran his fingers along the louvered vents for the cannon, the tear-shaped port seemingly too small to house the muzzle of a weapon. Adrenaline boiled through his arms and legs, breaking his movements into sharp jumps and harsh jerks. He grabbed the edge of the cockpit, hauling himself up onto the chin fairing. The Zvezda K-36D ejection seat sat behind an old-style dash of dials and rocker switch-gear. The instrument set was much closer to that of an A-10A than an F-15C.

Exactly as he remembered. Exactly.

The restraining straps were cinched against the seat. No helmet. No flight suit.

Not that he expected to find them here.

His own gear—where the hell was it?

Shit. Back on the helicopter. He'd forgotten it in the rush. Even if he didn't need the suit and helmet, he wanted the flight board. He'd taken it with him on every flight he'd ever made as a pilot, even the Russian Fulcrum spin. It was good luck.

"Major, the jamming station control panel is in the upper left-hand quadrant, below the angle-of-attack," said Wong. He popped the back of a small camera, quickly changing the film as he spoke. "Please examine it first. Information on the radar warning scope would likewise be beneficial. I have photographed the cockpit and the flight computer. I will now document the exterior hard points and other areas of interest."

Hack spun around, nearly kicking Wong in the face.

"I need my gear," he said. "It's in the helicopter. Get it."

"Your bag is on the apron there, where Sergeant Fernandez placed it," said Wong, gesturing.

"Good." Hack looked to his right. The hangar was open and unguarded. "The Iraqis must have their flight gear in the hangar. Come on."

"Please. We must complete our evaluation of the aircraft first," said the captain, refusing to clear off the ladder.

Hack stepped away and leapt off the airplane, holding the rifle in front of him for balance as he landed. It wasn't as far as he thought. His right leg buckled slightly, the knee he'd whacked before complaining, but he kept his balance, staggering a step ahead and then turning to run to Eugene, who was examining the underside of the wings.

"Not plumbed for air-to-air refueling," the British mechanic announced. That wasn't big news—almost no MiG-29's were. "Or for wing tanks. I'm not familiar with the mounting on points three and five; perhaps it is an Iraqi arrangement for unguided bombs."

"Forget all that," Hack told him. An Apache whizzed low overhead, drowning his words. He shouted as loud as he could. "Fuel. Is it fueled?"

"What?" said the mechanic.

"We need to fuel it!"

"Yes. Captain Wong wants me to examine the radar, and then the rest of the avionics."

"Fuel! Does it have fuel?"

The mechanic blinked, then pushed his hand over his bald head, perplexed.

"Fuel!" shouted Hack.

He pushed the man toward the plane, then began running toward the hangar. Short and squat, the building was made entirely of metal; it looked more like a civilian warehouse than a military hangar. Thick bands of smoke slithered from the dark interior. The heavy sulfuric odor made Preston cough as he ran. As he reached the door he pushed his rifle up. He couldn't see anything inside the building, but squeezed the trigger anyway, as if a random spray of bullets would guarantee his safety.

Nothing happened. He glanced down and realized he'd placed his finger not on the rifle trigger but on the grenade mechanism.

He coughed again, this time so hard that he had to drop to one knee to recover. But the air was even thicker here, the scent stifling. He rose slowly, telling himself to slow down.

A small fire burned about midway down the far side of the hangar, casting a reddish glow across the interior. Metal ramps and a small hand truck sat near the glow; a set of benches and lockers were lined against the wall.

A tractor was parked on his right. Hack sidled toward it, trying to hold back his coughs. A bomb trolley had been hooked to the back of the vehicle; two slim antiair missiles sat in its base.

Hack put his arm to his mouth, filtering the stench. Something moved on the floor a few feet from a workbench beyond the weapons carriage.

This time his finger was in the right place. Bullets ripped through the figure and ricocheted everywhere, the hangar reverberating with the automatic-weapon fire.

Preston coughed uncontrollably and threw himself down, rolling and starting to retch, his lungs and throat scratched by the toxic fumes of the smoldering fire. His nose and mouth felt like they had been filled with shavings from a metal lathe. Hack lost his hold on the gun and fell against the floor, stomach heaving.

He knew he had to stand up to breathe, but he wasn't sure if there were other Iraqis in the hangar, or even if he'd killed the man he'd aimed at. Finally he summoned his energy and jumped up, threw his hand over his face, and pumped his lungs against the fabric of his jumpsuit.

A man sprawled across the ground ten feet away. Hack froze, then realized the Iraqi wasn't moving. He could see the man's head glowing with the dim red light of the fire across the way.

A helmet. The pilot.

He edged toward the man, lungs pinching in his chest. He had to get outside and breathe.

The building's walls rattled with a nearby explosion. Hack reached down and grabbed the man's leg, hauling him backward toward the yawning blue light. He started slowly, then felt himself tripping. He managed to keep his balance long enough to reach the entrance, where he fell over backward. He whirled over, still coughing as the clean air hit his face. He gulped it, then reached back for the boot, pulling the Iraqi clear into the sunlight.

The dead pilot's fingers were wrapped around a pistol. He was fully dressed in flight gear and helmet. While his torso and limbs were intact, his nose and forehead looked more like a smashed pumpkin covered with red pulp than anything human. Part of the flight helmet was missing; the rest was cracked and fused to the man's skull.

Something warm touched Hack's shoulder. He flinched, but then realized it was Fernandez, the Delta soldier.

"I shot him," Hack said.

"I think a grenade got him, Major," said Fernandez. "Look at the helmet."

"Maybe," said Hack, though he knew he'd seen the man move. He dropped down, examining the flight suit. It didn't seem torn, though there were blood splatters all over it. The survival gear and belts, nicked here and there but seemingly sound, were thick with blood, already congealing into brown crust.

A helmet and mask. He'd have to go back into the hangar and find them. There must be a dressing station further back.

"Fuel's on its way, coming across the strip," yelled Eugene, running up to him and pointing across the field.

"Can you load missiles?" Hack asked.

"Missiles?"

"There's a pair in there, attached to a tractor. Can you get them on the plane?"

"I don't know."

"Hangar's on fire," Fernandez said.

"I know that," said Preston, running back into the building. He bunched the top of his jumpsuit up to cover his mouth, and tried to hold his breath as much as possible. He pointed to the tractor, hoping the others were following, then kept going, kicking his 203 on the floor as he ran.

There should be a rack of suits standing against the wall, lockers for personal gear.

Or maybe not. Maybe they used the buildings on the other side of the base.

No, he was thinking about this all wrong. It wasn't a real air base. It was more like a lone bus terminal, a solitary stop.

Might be no gear here at all then.

The fire licked across the row of benches at the left, blue flames circling a tank of some sort. The light waxed and waned, cycling from red to purple to blue, the fire seeming to die but then trickling back.

Three large trucks sat at the back of the building. Empty sacks sprawled on the floor near the far corner. Several workbenches and metal structures nearby looked like lockers. Hack moved toward the lockers, then saw that the sacks were men's bodies.

Something rumbled behind him. Hack whirled, expecting the building to come crashing down. But it was just the tractor—Eugene and Fernandez had managed to get it started.

Hack stepped over the bodies, looking for the suits or at least a helmet. The dead men were just workers or soldiers, of no use to him. There were large metal tool chests under the benches, and some old machinery that seemed like farming equipment. Tires were stacked against the wall, not far from where the fire was slowly working its way through a pile of rags or some other material.

As Hack turned to go back to the other side, his leg kicked something on the floor. The fire flared bright and he saw it was an oxygen mask, its long hose curled in a neat spiral. He scooped it up, and heard something pop behind him. Now there was plenty of light to see—the fire leapt into a can on the floor, exploding and flaring up the tires, firing along the lockers and climbing up the benches. Hack ran out of the hangar, feeling the heat as the flames suddenly found plenty of fuel to ignite.

"The plane! Get the plane out of the way! Away from the hangar! The fire!" he screamed.

Fernandez and Eugene had already hooked the front of the MiG up to the tractor. The plane jerked and screeched as it moved—the Fulcrum's parking brakes were obviously still set. Hack tucked the mask and hose beneath his arm and ran for the wing, hauling himself up over the trailing edge flap as the plane stuttered forward with a long, loud groan. He caught the back end of the canopy and threw the mask inside the cockpit, then squeezed himself around and down into the seat, his right leg catching on one of the panels as he fell in. He curled it back and beneath him as best he could, trying to orient himself.

So where was the brake?

His hands flailed against the left side of the cockpit of the unfamiliar plane. He couldn't remember a thing, not from the MiG he had flown in or the briefings.

The emergency extension for the landing gear was on the left, at the bottom of the panel near his knee.

His mind blanked. He couldn't have found the parking brake on a Chevy, let alone work a foreign airplane.

On the panel, on the panel.

Hack found the small, slender handle right above the

turn-and-slip indicator. He clawed at it, and the MiG rolled forward and then sideways, stopping abruptly. Unsure of himself again, not trusting his memory, he fumbled around the cockpit, looking for something else.

Wong appeared on the right wing, shouting.

They were sitting on the apron, safe, at least for now.

"The configuration appears to be the most primitive export model," said Captain Wong. "Do you concur?"

"Yeah, whatever," said Preston, pushing himself up. He pulled the oxygen hose out from under his leg, untangling himself in the process. He took the end and inserted it into the panel, then sat himself back down, getting his bearings now, remembering himself, his plan, his checklist.

He needed his flight board. Not for the few notes he'd scribbled—hell, they were useless now; he had all the important stuff memorized and he could, would remember it. But the cartoon, and Ecclesiastes, and most of all his dad's advice—couldn't fly without that.

Wisdom exceeds folly.

Do your best.

Don't be superstitious.

Hack turned his attention back to the plane. It had been outside the hangar, so the Iraqis might have already fueled it.

Power the instruments, find out.

Hack turned to the power panel on the right, began walking himself through the checklist he'd repeated on the flight from KKMC to the Delta base.

Power, number one. Switches set, check them front to back.

He remembered Lieutenant Romochka Dmitri Krainiye—"Harry" to his friends and Westerners—the Commie pilot who took him up at Kubinka. He had walked him through it step by step. Easy stuff.

They'd puffed that engine, though, starting off an external power source.

Do your best.

Hack looked at the voltmeter in front of his crotch.

He had a good battery. Hot shit.

What was next?

As his eyes rose across the rest of the instruments, he felt a twinge of vertigo, dizzy suddenly, the rush from the hangar catching up with him.

Do your best.

He remembered his dad saying that to him during a Little League game when he was walking to the plate, bases loaded.

He'd struck out.

Blinking and then rubbing his eyes, Hack stared at the gauge faces. He recognized the clock, an old-fashioned dial at the base of the panel. It was his anchor.

Compass at the top right. HUD, of course, slaved to the radar. Gear below it. Armament on his right—hard to reach in a dogfight, not natural.

No place for a critique.

Fuel gauge was a bar indicator with a flow gauge on the right side of the central panel. He'd had trouble keeping track of it during his flight at Kubinka—you had to stare at the damn thing to figure it out.

No fuel.

"Do you have power?" asked Wong.

"Yeah. Fuel it! Get us some juice. I can go!" he yelled to Wong, pushing up out of the seat. "Four thousand kilos, no more. The runway's damn short and I need it light."

Wong started to complain, but Hack pulled himself out, rolling off the plane to get the flight gear.

Flames licked out of the hangar.

He'd undress the dead pilot, use his own helmet.

Preston rolled over the side of the plane, intending to walk along the cowling, but slipping and going right to the ground. He hit awkwardly, kept his balance, ran to the dead man as a Hog whipped overhead, fifty feet off the runway. The ground shook with a massive explosion. An arm caught him as he began to fall.

"The Iraqis are sending reinforcements," said Captain Hawkins, pulling him up and yelling in his face as two Apaches crossed overhead. "Maybe tanks and helicopters. If you're going, you better make it fast."

13

Skull banked his plane south, cutting back over the line of hills that lay to the east of Splash. Smoke curled from a dozen places as he flew, the battle sorting itself into several messy knots. Closest to him was the hangar and apron area, where the MiG was being worked on perhaps seventy yards from the hangar. A Pave Hawk passed between it and the edge of the runway, .50-caliber bullets spitting from its doorway. An RAF Chinook skittered from the hangar area toward the buildings on the northwestern end of the complex. Apaches zipped around the buildings, peppering them and the surrounding emplacements with rockets and gunfire. Smoke furled everywhere, in every sort of permutation— gray wisps and thick black clouds, red-tinted mushrooms and diaphanous white scarves.

The commandos had entered the buildings. From what Knowlington could decipher from the excited communications, neither team had found any trace of their quarry. The SAS men were using mobile infrared radar units and other detectors. To lessen the chance of hitting their own men, the Apaches were in direct communication with the helicopters, but the gunships were not exactly subtle—every so often their chins would erupt in smoke and blue flame, and part of the buildings would implode.

A group of F-16's, their services not needed for the initial assault, had diverted to nearby secondary targets, including a small ammo dump or bunker area just below the runway. They were already en route home, leaving three A-10's—Skull and his wingman, Antman, along with Dixon—to cover contingencies. The scheduled escort flight of four Navy F-14's had been reduced to two, apparently because of mechanical problems; the planes had just relieved the F-15's and would remain to escort Hack and the MiG back.

As Skull banked west, he saw a glint on the road about ten miles away, up toward the river and a highly populated area. He told Dixon and Antman to stay in a wheeling orbit over the airfield, then nudged his stick. As he did, he noticed a cloud of dust where the highway should be.

Splash controller came over the circuit, reporting that one of the Apaches had seen a column of vehicles and possibly a helicopter approaching. Someone else came on the line, ignoring the controller's attempt to keep them quiet. By the time the circuit cleared, Skull had changed course and identified targets in the dust cloud:

A dozen vehicles, including at least three light tanks or self-propelled guns and a jeep, coming along the highway toward Splash.

"Add two transport helicopters," he told the Splash controller as the helos caught up to the column.

They were at very low altitude, slowing as they caught the column. Mi-8 Hips, probably, large transport types that occasionally carried rockets in side packs along the cabin.

Skull studied the area beyond the helicopters, expecting escorts or other Hips to appear. He suspected there would be more—an entire formation of Mi-8's and Mi-24 Hind gunships and Fishbeds, everything Saddam could throw at them.

Nothing.

They'd have to swing with the highway at a bend three miles away. Get the lead vehicles there with Mavericks while the F-14's splashed the helicopters.

On beam for that.

"I'm at two o'clock," Dixon snapped as Skull alerted his flight. "I have the Hip."

"Negative," Skull told him. "Let the Navy boys take the helicopters. Stand off and let them in. We'll get the column as it clears that bend northeast of the airport."

Devil Two swooped ahead, well out of formation.

"Dixon? What the hell are you doing?" he said, flipping the transmit button off quickly and listening for an answer.

"Dixon, you're supposed to be east where I told you to orbit. Acknowledge. Dixon! Dixon!"

14

The seeker head in the Hog's Sidewinder missile growled at him, anxious to launch. It had locked on the helicopter's hot turbine engines from nearly eight miles away—much too far to fire and guarantee a hit.

BJ had done this all before. He pushed on toward the Iraqi helicopter, keeping the large angled exhaust square in the middle of his windshield, a juicy target for his missile.

The helicopter skittered on obliviously, flanking a line of dark tan vehicles, dust billowing behind. BJ goosed his throttle; barely twenty feet off the ground, he nudged over three hundred nautical miles an hour.

The Sidewinder growl deepened, its target tantalizingly close—six miles, five and a half, five.

Something flared on his right, something on the ground firing at him. His helmet jangled with static, then a voice.

Knowlington, ordering him to stand down, back off, get the hell out of the way—a Tomcat was targeting the helicopters.

Static swallowed the voice, then silence replaced the static. The helo was dead-on now, four miles away.

Dixon took a breath. He pushed the trigger and an AIM-9 whipped off the double launcher on his left wing tip. A string of smoke curled through the air as it nosed down toward the Hip, which jerked violently around, finally realizing it was in trouble.

Dixon watched as the missile sailed straight over the helicopter, flaring as it ignited in one of the vehicles beyond.

As he started to curse, he realized he was about to fly into the rising ground ahead. He pulled his stick back just enough to keep from scraping the sand, and at the same time reached to switch to cannon. At inside two miles from his target he slammed his rudder hard, pushing the targeting cue dead onto the Hip's tail. But the helicopter moved to his right, and Dixon was so low and had lost so much momentum, it was difficult to stay with it. All he could do was take out another truck—he lit the Gat and erased a jeep, bullets pouncing on the soft metal of the vehicle's body. He worked his rudder and slid his aim into the nose of a self-propelled gun, getting off a half-second burst before losing the angle as well as some of his altitude. As he started to recover, the other helicopter appeared almost overhead. Dixon avoided the temptation to try to target it; the shot would have been nearly impossible and would have cost what little he had left of his momentum besides. He banked right, starting to pick up speed, and saw the helicopters off on his right—along with two dark hulls streaking to join them.

Not the F-14's, which must still be a good distance off. Not the other Hogs, which for the moment he'd lost track of.

Hinds, serious gunfighters that carried antiair missiles as well as ground-attack weapons.

No match for a Hog, though. He'd proven that in the first days of the war.

Dixon put his nose toward the biggest shadow, still a good seven or eight miles off. The second Sidewinder, his last, growled from its wing-tip rail.

He waited ten long, long seconds, closing to inside five miles before firing. Then he lined up on the second gunship as it broke south just out of range of his cannon.

A single word broke through the static in his helmet, as if it were fighting its way through the circuits and wires. Short and guttural, it had a sharp snap that could only come from Colonel Knowlington. Before the meaning of the actual word registered, Dixon knew it was a warning:

"Missile!"

15

Becky Rosen bolted upright from the cot. Stones had been placed on her body, heavy weights that made it difficult to move. The gray light turned purple and the warm air froze.

"BJ! BJ!" she shouted.

The empty tent remained silent. Slowly, she caught her breath, senses returning to normal.

It was only a dream, she told herself, curling her arms across her breasts.

A dream, a bad dream.

Rosen started to pull the covers back over her, then realized she was late for duty. She bolted from the bed, the weights still damping her movements.

He's okay, she told herself, pushing on her boots. She tried thinking of everything she had to do, tried imagining what she might have for breakfast, tried remembering her uncle's junkyard, but the light in the tent remained a dark tinge not unlike the color of dried blood.

16

Skull fired the Maverick at the knot of men who had jumped from the truck and set up the shoulder-launched missiles. Something flared in the targeting screen just as the AGM launched; Knowlington punched the transmit button, barking another warning, though he couldn't be sure the Iraqis had actually fired a SAM. He caught a glimpse of Dixon's Hog wheeling in the sky over the Iraqis eight miles ahead, then lost it, his attention drawn back to the Maverick screen, where he had to target the lead vehicle in the convoy to stop it.

It was too late to do anything more for Dixon. The kid had left his butt wide open. Luck might save him, but it was too late for anything else.

Why the hell hadn't he done what he was told?

Knowlington locked the AGM-65's targeting cursor on the armored personnel carrier following the lead jeep, and fired. As the missile clunked off the rail, Antman said there were more helicopters coming almost due south from across the river, a bit over ten miles away. Skull cut back, banking in a wide orbit south of the Iraqi convoy so he could sort out the situation. His wingman approached the convoy from the southwest; he reported that the colonel's two missiles had hit their targets.

"Smoke and shit all over the place," said the wingman, whom Skull could see in the left corner of his windscreen.

"Column stopped?"

"Not all of it," said Antman. "I have a good view of two tanks."

"Get 'em, then wheel back south. I'll come up more or less in the same orbit. I'm on your back," added Skull, pushing his Hog around to turn back north. He had two Mavericks and a pair of cluster bombs left, along with his gun and the Sidewinders.

He watched a Maverick drop from Antman's wing, fuming away. The Iraqis were still coming. The troop helicopters were still with them.

The F-14's were having trouble targeting the helos—the helicopters were apparently so low that even the vaunted long-range radars in the Tomcats couldn't isolate them in the ground clutter.

The helicopters coming south were larger though much farther away. He saw them as he began banking, spiders skipping over the ground, cutting a vector toward Splash.

Mi-24 Hinds. Deadly bastards that combined the firepower of Apaches with the troop-carrying capability of Black Hawks.

So where the hell were the damn Tomcats?

And where was Dixon?

"Shit!" yelled Antman as something flared from the spider on the right. Steam erupted from the other helicopter, and red streaks filled the sky.

They were targeting the SAS team holding the highway with long-range air-to-ground missiles.

There were a dozen men there, no match for the brawny helicopters. Knowlington was just about ten miles from the helicopters. Out of range for the Sidewinders.

Stinking helicopters ought to be out of range too, but

the bastards were really going at it, lighting their rockets now. The ground erupted with furious explosions.

He pushed his throttle, coaxing the Hog for more speed. His elbows sagged against his body, and his groin muscles cramped as the Hinds tracked toward their prey.

Was this why he'd taken the mission, his last mission, to go out a failure, let his guys die?

Skull slammed his stick, angry at himself—not for failing, but for the bullshit self-pity. Remorse didn't mean jack to the poor bastards on the ground; it was useless, as useless and ultimately destructive as drinking.

He was closing the distance, but it wasn't going to be enough. The Sidewinders had trouble spotting the baffled heat signatures of the gunships, especially with the rockets acting as decoys.

Skull glanced at the Maverick screen. The targeting cursor sat just under the fat rotor at the top of the helicopter on the right.

Nail it?

With an air-to-ground missile?

In range. And shit, the damn helicopter was only ten feet off the ground. It wasn't going anywhere.

No way.

Mavs couldn't be confused by the flares, or ECMs for that matter.

No fucking way.

By the time the debate played out in Skull's mind, he had already fired the first Maverick at the chopper. The second clicked off the rail for the other Hind a half-breath later.

The solid-propellant rocket motors that powered the two missiles had been designed for reliability and ease of handling. While they weren't exactly slow, they propelled the AGMs at less than half the speed of a typical air-to-air missile. Likewise, the guidance system in the Mavericks had been optimized for its intended targets—tanks, which rarely moved faster than thirty miles an hour, and were hardly ever found off the ground.

On the other hand, the Maverick's guidance system

might be rated more accurate than that of many weapons, and once locked could not be easily confused. In fact, there was no reason, at least in theory, why the missiles could not hit something hovering aboveground, so long as it stayed more or less put.

Which the helicopters did, until nearly the last millisecond. Then the pilot in the lead Hind realized the thick splinter that had materialized on the right side of his cockpit glass was not a crack but a missile coming for him. He pushed his helicopter hard to the left, kicking flares and spinning his heat signature away.

The maneuver would have worked perfectly had Skull launched a Sidewinder. Here the Maverick merely skipped its nose down a little steeper, slightly increasing the speed at which its three-hundred-pound payload smashed through the armored windscreen of the weapons-system operator's cabin. The missile continued through at an angle, obliterating the crewman and carrying off a good hunk of the pilot's control panel as it smashed its way out of the aircraft.

It did not explode, and in fact the Hind continued to fly, though now without the benefit of control. The chopper shot straight up at its top speed of nearly 2,500 feet per minute. Its tail whipped around as the main blades pulled the craft onto its back. It stuttered for a second, drifting like a leaf caught in a steady wind. Then slowly it began to sink toward the earth, its tail circling as it plummeted to a fiery crash.

In contrast, the warhead on the second Maverick not only hit precisely where the targeting cursor had sent it, but detonated as well, obliterating the upper cabin area and engines and initiating a fireball that flashed over the entire helicopter. The flames continued to burn as the helo fell nearly straight downward, its charred skeleton neatly depositing its ashes in a small heap.

By that time, Knowlington had pushed east to drop his bombs on the elements of the Iraqi convoy that had managed to get around the vehicle he'd destroyed. He also realized why the Tomcats were late—they had just nailed a MiG-21 that had been scrambled to assist the Iraqi counterattack.

What he didn't know, though, was where Dixon was.

17

Dixon hit his flares and dove for the desert, zigging hard enough to pull six or seven g's as he tried to evade the shoulder-launched missile. It clawed for his tail like an animal groping in the dark; he flew like a machine, working the stick and rudder with sharp precision. He didn't feel fear—he didn't feel anything, just flew.

A white cigarette sailed fifty yards from his canopy; he glanced at it, then bucked his nose in its direction and kicked out more flares, calculating that the Iraqis would have launched a pair of the missiles and the second would be closer to his tail.

They hadn't had time. The first missile continued on, its self-destruct mechanism apparently defective; Dixon caught another glimpse of it arcing toward a line of gray buildings near the river. The Iraqis would undoubtedly blame the deaths it caused on the Americans, pretending that the Allies were targeting civilians with their weapons.

To Dixon, the distinctions between civilians and combatants no longer made any sense. There was only the war, only the job to be done. He pushed his Hog into a wide bank, reorienting himself. He'd flown far north; a sizable Iraqi town was laid out below his right wing. A few days before on the ground he had seen a similar town almost as if it were an isolated outpost in Wisconsin, where he'd grown up. Now he saw it merely as something he flew over, a place where an antiaircraft gun began lobbing shells behind him. Sighted manually and too light to be a threat, the gun's bullets pointed him back toward his target.

The static in his radio flared again. It was another warning, this time from Coyote, the AWACS plane monitoring the section.

"Devil Two, break! Break! Break!" shouted the controller in a hoarse voice as his words were once more consumed in a cacophony of electronic rustling. Dixon heard "MiG-21" and began tucking south, assuming that was the most logical direction the controller would have given him. As he made his cut, his warning gear tripped over an Iraqi Jay Bird radar, trying to get its sticky fingers on him. The warning cleared, but Dixon punched chaff anyway, rolling back toward the battlefield.

His headphones had gone quiet again. Neither Skull nor Antman answered his hail.

He looked over at the com panel. Something was definitely wrong with his radio; the staticky chatter that ordinarily provided background listening as he flew had faded into dead silence. He clicked through different frequencies, retrieving nothing. He switched back, broadcasting to Coyote though he couldn't be sure he was sending. Calm and slow, his voice nonetheless sounded strange inside his head, as if the radio's failure had affected his own sense of hearing.

"Devil Two is experiencing radio problems. If you're hearing me, I can transmit but not receive. Repeat, I can't hear a word you're saying."

He clicked off the mike button, checking altitude and speed—3,500 feet aboveground, level flight, 285 knots, nosing south by southwest. Splash was on his left; he had

a straight line to the black smoke rising from the Iraqi column and the splashed helicopters. The ruined Hinds sat in
heaps just before the highway. One of the transport helicopters, its rotors turning, was disgorging men near the
wrecks. Beyond them, scattered near and on the road, were
the Iraqi vehicles and troops that had been racing to
Splash's aid.

An A-10 dove toward the rear of the column. Bullets
spewed from its mouth, red and gray and black lightning
striking the earth. Steam hissed from the desert where it
struck. A fireball followed, exploding about fifty feet off
the ground as the Hog cleared and banked south. A few
hundred yards away, an Iraqi helicopter—seemingly untouched, though it must have been targeted by a missile—
rolled over in the air and folded into the ground, flames
shooting out from the side.

Dixon repeated his can't-hear-ya call on the squadron
frequency, but again got no response. He checked his fuel
situation, and saw he was about two pounds away from hitting bingo.

18

Hawkins ducked as one of the Apaches flashed overhead, hustling toward the escalating firefight out on the highway east of the airfield. Distant explosions shook the ground. The Pave Hawk that had deposited him circled back over the road below the southern end of the enemy base, the door gunner occasionally firing at the last defenders still holding out there.

One of the buildings the SAS had attacked had been secured. The other was surrounded, and an SAS interpreter was trying to get the last defenders to surrender. The clipped radio communications gave no clue about the missing commandos they'd come for. The heavy resistance didn't mean much, one way or another.

Burns and his men had captured the Iraqi fuel truck without resistance. Failing to get it started, they had pulled and pushed it from its bunker by hand, muscling it across the runway. It was fully loaded and the going was excruciatingly slow.

Finally, Wong and Fernandez took the tractor they had used to pull the MiG and drove out to the fuel truck, wheeling behind it and pushing it toward the MiG. In the meantime, Eugene and Preston fussed around the plane, getting it ready and even trying to load a missile onto its wing.

They're going to pull it off, Hawkins realized. Tight-assed Major Preston is actually going to fly the goddamn plane out of Iraq.

What in God's name were the odds against that? Talk about stinkin' luck.

Hot damn.

Something moved in the ditch beyond the runway apron beyond the MiG. The plane's landing gear obscured it, made it invisible—but Hawkins was already running for it, his SAW tight against his side.

It took ten long strides to pull parallel with the nose of the MiG. Two more strides, three, and he had the top of the ditch in view.

Empty.

But he knew he hadn't imagined it. He kept running. The truck, prodded unevenly by the tractor, heaved forward on his left. One of the British paratroopers coaxing it alongside was laughing. Burns was holding onto the door, talking with the driver, helping him steer.

Nothing in the ditch. Nothing.

He kept running, spotting another trench ten feet beyond the first, this one parallel to the runway.

Empty, except for three sacks of cement.

Men. A gun.

The SAW burst, then clicked empty. One of the bags of cement imploded. Burns fell off the truck.

The Iraqi at the far end of the trench stood with a long spear, jostling its pointed nose.

A javelin against a fuel truck?

Hawkins threw his bulletless gun down, still ten yards from the trench. One of the SAS men was grabbing for a weapon, but no one had started to fire.

Seven yards, five. Not a javelin, an RPG-7 or something similar. The Iraqi was screwing the propellant cylinder into the head, jamming it into the launcher muzzle, ramming it against the ground to steady his shot.

Hawkins screamed as he leapt into the ditch. A small bee whizzed over his head and another below his leg. The rocket flared inches from his eye. His right hand burned and something wet covered his face.

Then a fist punched him in the side. Hawkins threw his elbow in the direction of the blow, pushed up, and saw a blur in the shape of a rifle about a foot from his belly. He lunged for it, falling into the man holding it. Three bullets shot from the gun as they struggled. Hawkins managed to push his body into the Iraqi, pinning him against the side of the trench. He kicked his foot back as hard as he could against the man's leg, continuing until he could wrestle the gun free. He jerked it around and smashed it against the Iraqi. Then he sprang away, twisting to get his bearings. As he did, he saw a pipe roll from the top of the trench to the bottom near his foot.

By the time his conscious mind processed the fact that the pipe was not a pipe but a grenade, Hawkins had already grabbed hold of it. In the same motion he tossed it skyward. As it left his fingers he thought how incredibly lucky he must be that it hadn't gone off.

Then he realized that he had thrown it in the direction of the tanker truck.

In the next moment, it exploded. Hawkins had hunkered down, but could still feel the impact. Pieces of shrapnel and rock rained against the back and side of his body armor. He smashed his hand against the trench in anger, then rose, pushing away the body of a dead Iraqi that had fallen over his legs, struggling to get up and see the runway.

The tanker sat in front of the MiG, thirty yards away, intact. With his customary presence of mind, Wong had continued pushing it forward, while Hawkins and the others dealt with the Iraqis and their antitank weapon. The grenade had landed on the runway, but its shrapnel had missed the vehicles.

Not Burns, though. Hawkins pulled himself and walked to the SAS sergeant, whose body lay at the edge of the concrete. He'd been hit in the neck and legs and face; at least one of the holes had been caused by the Iraqi gunner and not the grenade, but it would have been difficult to tell which one was which, much less which one was fatal.

Hawkins knelt down. Burns lay faceup. The flap of the sergeant's breast pocket was open. Hawkins saw the back of the photograph Burns had shown him yesterday. Five kids and a wife who thought an afternoon in an amusement park was the time of their lives.

They always would now.

Blood trickled toward the photo. Hawkins reached down and took it out gingerly, holding it up as one of Burns's men ran to him.

"Iraqis got him?" asked the man.

Hawkins just frowned at him, handing him the picture.

"Let's get that fucking airplane the hell out of here," he said, starting after the truck.

19

Major Preston had just climbed back into the cockpit and turned to check where the fuel truck was when the grenade exploded. He ducked, losing his balance and nearly falling over the side. He slammed his side and back against a sharp piece of the fairing; his kidney hurt so badly he thought he'd been hit by the grenade. He crumpled against the seat, disoriented and confused, head swirling as if he'd taken nine or ten negative g's. Somehow he got upright and tried to shake the black cowl away from his head; he didn't dare look at his body, still thinking he'd been wounded by the exploding grenade.

I'll fly no matter what, he thought to himself, and he felt his side with his hands. His fingers slipped lightly over the fabric, then pushed against the folds, pressing finally against his back.

He hadn't been hit.

The truck continued toward the plane. Hack climbed out of the cockpit to help refuel, extending his legs to the

ladder. An Apache whipped overhead from the other side
of the runway; for a second it looked like its skids would
ram into the airplane and he ducked, cringing. The helicopter pulled away at the last instant and Hack tightened
his grip as the wash rattled around him. He stepped back,
toeing the step, then lost his balance as he tried to move
too quickly to the ground.

He twisted as he fell, smashing his left wrist and hand
against one of the ladder's metal steps. A fresh burst of
machine-gun fire somewhere nearby froze him, and once
more he thought he'd been shot.

He pulled himself away from the ladder slowly, punch-
drunk. Hack felt a flash of queasiness in his stomach. His
left wrist hung off at an angle, a bone probably broken. The
thin layer of flesh below his thumb grew purple as he
watched. The rest of his forearm quickly began to swell.
The pain began to multiply wildly, a puff adder suddenly
excited. The wound's poison paralyzed him. Preston
pushed his head down, flexing his shoulder and back muscles as if they might somehow take over for the injured
bones and ligaments.

And then he forced himself to his feet and away from
the plane, yelling to Wong and the others on the truck that
they had to hurry. He turned toward the hangar, consumed
with the next problem, flight gear.

He could wear his own speed suit with the fudged g-suit
hose connectors his survival experts had supplied, but it
would be infinitely better to take the gear the dead pilot
was wearing. Preston ran to the figure he had dragged from
the hangar. He bent his head away from the mess that had
been the man's face. Using only his right hand, he began
to undress him, pulling off the bib-type outer flight suit.
Despite the bloody crust, neither the bib nor the g suit
below appeared damaged. The legs were covered with
dark black figures, a sort of freehand graffiti that seemed
more like a superstitious scrawl than a mark of ownership.
Preston stopped and undid his own boots, then stripped to
his cotton long johns. He tried to use his left hand to pull
off the man's boots, and his wrist throbbed so badly he

ended up using his knees and even briefly his head for leverage as he finished stripping the Iraqi.

The back of the g suit was stained black. The pilot's intestines had released a stream of shit as he died.

Hack pulled the suit away from the sodden underwear, gingerly rolling the pants legs up with his right hand before standing to slide them up. The Iraqi pilot had been about two inches shorter than Preston and five pounds lighter; the suit snugged very tightly in the groin, but the top fit well enough for him to move his shoulders freely. He pulled his boots back on, grabbed the mask he had found and left nearby, and then took one last look at the helmet.

Broken beyond use.

He went to his bag and ripped it open, scooping out his own liner and helmet, fitting them on as he ran back toward the plane.

The explosions in the distance had stopped, as had most of the gunfire. He heard a few soft clicks as he snugged the helmet down, then nothing.

Eugene had placed the AA-11 antiair missile below the wing but not attached it. Hack ran to the knot of men helping fuel the plane, pulling at one and then another before finding the RAF mechanic.

"The missile," he yelled, pointing. "Get the missile on. It'll help."

Eugene shook his head and started to say something. Preston pushed the mechanic in the direction of the weapon. "Do it! Do it!" he shouted, then ran around the front of the plane, looking to see if anything obvious was out of place. It wasn't exactly an FAA inspection, but the plane was there, all there. He touched the afterburner nozzles, their gray housing designed to lower IR signatures, then ran around the tailplane, around the wing—navigation light cracked by shrapnel—and back to the ladder. Eugene was stooped under the wing examining the hard points; he had not mounted the missile.

"You need help? What?" Hack asked.

"The missile is irrelevant," said Wong, pulling at his shoulder.

"Not to me," said Hack.

A pair of Chinooks shot overhead, their heavy rotors shaking the earth. Wong started speaking nonetheless.

"It is an AA-7 Aphid, not an AA-11. The type is thoroughly understood. Even if we can install it, the missile will only add needlessly to your weight, and time is short. You won't need it," added Wong.

The captain was right.

"Is it fueled?"

"Four thousand kilos, as you directed. That will cut your range—"

"It's fine. I'm not going to California." Hack pushed the ladder back against the plane. His left wrist collapsed but he ignored the pain, shoving with his shoulder.

Wong helped, but grabbed him as he started up.

"Your left hand?" Wong asked.

"Banged my wrist."

"Can you fly?"

Hack shrugged. "Let's see if I can get the damn thing started. Get the fuel truck out of the way."

Still holding onto Hack's flight vest, Wong put his other hand around Hack's wrist and squeezed. Even if it hadn't been injured, the pressure would have hurt—but Hack did his best not to acknowledge the pain. He pulled his arm and body away, and went up the ladder.

By now the cockpit seemed almost familiar, the ten-degree-canted seat a favorite La-Z-Boy recliner. The parachute harness attached with a single clasp at the chest; Hack had trouble with it, struggling to position his body and cinch it at the same time. His left hand was so worthless he kept it in his lap as he donned the oxygen mask and made the connections on the left side of the cockpit. He checked the brake, took a breath, and began working through the engine start procedure.

Do your best.

His flight board. He didn't have it.

Screw it now. He had to go, go, go.

Designed from the very beginning to work under primitive conditions, the MiG-29 had an admirably austere feel that would not go unappreciated by an A-10A aficionado. Though a completely different aircraft with an entirely different mission, the Fulcrum had also been engineered to rely on mechanical systems, not cutting-edge computers and fly-by-wire gizmos. One of those systems was the doors that closed off the engine inlets to avoid ingesting debris when taking off. Another was the auxiliary power unit, which sent a big breath of compressed air across the left Tumanski R-33D turbofan, spinning it until it coughed and clicked and surged.

And died.

If Hack's left wrist hadn't been sprained already, he would have sprained it when he slammed it against the throttle bar, pissed that he had come this far only to fail. He screamed the whole way through a second start sequence, but couldn't get the engine to kick again—had no power, in fact, on the panel.

From the beginning, he told himself. Start over. Slow.

He was already trying to think up a way to have the tractor puff the Tumanski when the plane's auxiliary unit managed to wind the power plant with a small huff of air. This time it coughed loud and whirled into a steady roar, everything vibrating wildly.

Hack checked the rpm—sturdy, in the middle of the gauge, but what exactly was the spec?

He'd blanked, but the number didn't matter. He got the next engine up anyway. The rumble was firm; there was no doubt he was in the green.

Was there?

The dials were all over the place—he was sitting in an F-15 with instruments from an A-10 that had been arranged by a schizophrenic engineer.

Weren't all engineers schizophrenic?

Go over the restraints again, check the flight gear, don't fuck up. Oxygen—something was wrong, because he wasn't getting anything out of the mask.

As he leaned over to examine the panel near his left elbow, he realized for the first time that the hose had been split between one of the coils. He'd need to repair it. He pulled it apart, then saw it wasn't just split—shrapnel or bullets had blown a series of holes clear through.

He could just tape it.

No time.

Fly low.

F-14's expected him at thirty thousand feet.

Tough shit on that. Stay at five thousand feet, lower.

Get nailed by antiair. Forget the Iraqis—the Allies would nail him.

He would fly low, though not quite so low as that; it made sense. But it didn't make sense to fly without an oxygen mask since he had his own, even if its hose fitting was only a kludge. As the MiG shook against its brakes, Preston loosened his restraints and leaned over the side of the plane. Wong and Hawkins were standing a short distance away with another member of the Delta team, both trying to listen to a single com set.

"My bag!" he screamed. "My bag! My bag!"

They couldn't hear him over the whine of the engines. Finally Eugene saw him and ran toward him.

"My mask, my mask," he shouted, holding up the one he had taken from the Iraqis. "Get the whole bag! The whole bag! I want my board too."

Might as well.

"My bag! Shit!" he screamed.

The engines were too loud. Eugene ran to get the ladder.

Hawkins and Wong finally glanced up.

"My bag!" Hack shouted to them. "I need the mask. And the board."

Wong pointed toward the far end of the runway. At first, Hack didn't understand what the hell he meant. Finally, he turned around.

One of the Chinooks had crashed there and was on fire.

20

"Devil Leader, this is Splash Control. Buildings are secure and exfiltration is beginning. We have another difficulty. Please acknowledge."

Skull had just turned his nose back toward Splash. A billow of black smoke rose between two Apaches. One of the Chinooks had crashed after being hit by gunfire.

Knowlington listened to the terse explanation, then assured Splash Control that he would stay nearby in case he was needed.

He had his own problems, though. The Iraqi relief column had been neutralized. Three of the helicopters were burning on the ground and the fourth had scrambled away to the west. But Dixon was still lost and not answering hails.

As Skull tried to reach the AWACS to request a fix on his squadron mate, a dark wing crossed behind the smoke wisping from the carcass of a self-propelled gun at the far end of the highway. He clicked onto the squadron frequency, hailing Dixon and asking why the hell he hadn't responded.

He didn't get an answer.

"Antman, you see him?" Knowlington asked his wingman.

"Uh, I got him at, uh, call it five miles, four and a half. He's heading south of the highway, just passing that open truck I hit with the gun."

"I don't think he has a radio," Knowlington said. "Let's catch up."

"Four."

The two Hogs spread out in the sky, Devil Leader looping ahead and Four angling tighter, aiming to make sure Dixon noticed at least one of them as he flew. Dixon saw Antman first, wagging his wings slightly, then starting to climb toward his altitude. By the time Skull swept back around and drew alongside, Antman had pulled close enough to use hand signals.

"Says he's all right except for the radio, if I'm reading his sign language right," said Antman. "Got to work on his penmanship."

By even the most optimistic calculation, Dixon would be well into his reserve fuel by now. He had to get straight home, and he needed someone to run with him.

Skull knew it had to be Antman; there was no way he would leave the kid here to take out the MiG by himself. But shepherding a stricken Hog home wasn't going to be a picnic either.

Antman was a good, decent pilot with a strong sense of what he was about. But he was still a kid. Dixon was still a kid. They'd have to fly more than two hundred miles before putting down; they'd have to do so over hostile territory at slow speed and relatively low altitude.

Skull wanted to go with them—not because he didn't trust them, and certainly not because he didn't think they could do it, but because he felt as if his presence would somehow protect them, somehow balance against the unpredictable contingencies and chaos of war.

They weren't kids, not really. But he felt as if he ought to be there, to protect them.

Hubris. As if he were omnipotent, not an old goat with eyes and hands that were steadily slowing.

But that was the way he felt.

"Dixon's going to be low on fuel," Knowlington told the lieutenant. "You take him south. I'll hang back and cover Splash."

"Check six, Colonel," said Antman, wishing him luck with the time-honored slogan of goodwill—and caution.

"Yeah," said Skull. "Check six."

21

Dixon answered Antman's thumbs-up with one of his own, then settled onto the course heading he had flashed with his fingers a few moments earlier. The other Hog edged further off his wing, though it remained so close, BJ thought Antman could hear him if he popped the canopy and yelled.

That was the kind of thing Shotgun would suggest. Hell, it was the kind of thing Shotgun might try.

O'Rourke was a damn good flight leader, Dixon thought as he matched Antman's slow, steady climb toward the border. He'd laid out the mission well, kept BJ aware of the situation, responded to his own problems in a way that guaranteed the mission would succeed. He acted like a goof-off sometimes, but that was just an act.

The man William James Dixon truly admired was the old-dog colonel who'd put Antman on his wing as his personal guide dog. Knowlington was a gray-hair, but there he was, circling back to cover the Splash team, moving as methodically as a freshly refurbished grandfather clock.

Not long ago, Dixon thought guys like Skull hung around either out of vanity or in hopes of catching an adrenaline rush. Now he realized it wasn't either. After a while, after you went through enough shit, you didn't feel any more adrenaline—maybe you didn't feel anything. You did your job, and you kept doing it because that was your job. If your job was to be the gray-haired geezer who knew everything, you did it.

And *his* job?

His job was to get home, see Becky, feel her next to him.

As he passed through seven thousand feet, Dixon spotted a small group of clouds dead ahead. The furls on the left side reminded him of a kid's face; it became impossible not to think of the boy who'd saved his life.

Why had the kid done it? Dixon had saved him a short while before, but still, to jump on a grenade?

The cloud disappeared as Dixon approached. Perhaps it hadn't even been there at all, for the sky before him was about as clear as he'd ever seen in his life. The Iraqi desert, bleak and cold, spread out below him. A thick pall hung over the horizon to his left—oil fires in Kuwait, most likely. Antiair artillery rose up about a mile away, futilely searching the sky for something to hit.

Why was he here? He could have gone home to America; Knowlington and the others had made that clear.

The only answer Dixon had was the unlimited sky and the furling clouds on the ground, the feel of his fingers curling around his stick, the cold scratch of fatigue at his eyes. There were no answers to any of his questions about the kid, about his mother, about himself. There was just gravity and the force of the engines, pushing him along.

That, and Becky's body folded against his.

BJ checked his instruments, then corrected slightly to keep in Antman's close shadow.

22

Math had never been among Shotgun's favorite subjects. While he was unable to avoid numbers and equations completely, he nonetheless made it a practice whenever possible to treat them with the sort of disdain he might show a month-old French fry.

His loathing of basic arithmetic could not, however, alter the fact that his fuel gauge was taking a steady and dramatic plunge toward negative integers. And it didn't take a quadratic equation to calculate that there was no way in hell that he was going to make it back to Saudi Arabia, much less the Home Drome, on his rapidly dwindling supply.

It didn't make sense—he was flying on one engine and ought to be using a lot less fuel than normal, which meant the camel's hump ought to be at least half full.

Unless, of course, some of those Iraqi gunners had managed to nick his fuel tanks just right. He had no warning lights and the plane seemed to be flying just fine—but there was no arguing with the fuel gauge; Shotgun had to tank, and soon.

A pair of MH-130's had been tasked with refueling the helicopters, and a Pave Low with a buddy pack was also part of the package as an emergency backup. Unfortunately, the drogue-and-basket system they used was incompatible with the boomer receptacle the Hog had in its nose. But as he glanced at his notes for the nearest tanker track, Shotgun wondered if there might be some way to make the system work.

If the A-10 had had an autopilot, he might have set it, then popped the canopy and crawled on the nose, stuffed the hose inside the open fuel door, and told them to pump away.

Fortunately, Coyote, the AWACS controller monitoring the area, had a better idea.

"We have a KC-135 on an intercept to you," said the controller. "Call sign is Budweiser."

"What I am talking about," said Shotgun, though Budweiser's position left him somewhat less enthusiastic—he'd have to climb ten thousand feet and jog sixty miles west to catch the straw. He turned onto the course, hoping for the best—and ignoring the math, which showed that even if he did manage the climb on one engine, he'd run out of fuel about the time the KC-135 came into sight.

Budweiser, fortunately, was a typical member of the tanker community, the unsung but well-hung fraternity of guys who never let anyone go home thirsty. The crew had already crunched the throttle to accelerate toward the stricken Hog, passing over enemy territory.

"Devil One, we understand you have a fuel emergency," the pilot radioed as soon as Shotgun dialed in the frequency. "State your situation."

"Pretty much bone-dry. Got a problem with one of my sumps, it looks like. I think I'm leakin' like a water bucket without a bottom," replied O'Rourke. "Worst thing is, I'm down to my last bag of Twizzlers."

"This Shotgun? Shit. I'm always bailing you out."

"I was countin' on it, Bobby Boy," Shotgun told the

pilot. "Otherwise I wouldn't have let Saddam shoot up the tanks."

"Thought those Hogs were impenetrable."

"What I'm talking about," answered Shotgun. "But that don't mean they don't leak a little."

"Stay on your course and altitude, we'll come down to you," said the pilot.

"Just what I like—a beer guy who delivers," said Shotgun. "And hey, you still owe me ten bucks from that poker game."

"Watch it, or I'll tell my boomer to miss on his first try," joked the pilot, referring to the crewman who handled the refueling gear.

"Won't work," said Shotgun. "I owe him fifty."

23

Skull lowered his head, giving himself a moment to gather himself under the guise of checking his map.

He remembered a mission, flying a late-model Phantom F-4 out of Alaska, where he'd intercepted a Tupolev Tu-95 Bear—standard Cold War show, part of an ongoing project at the time where each side tried to outchicken the other. Except this one was different. The Bear was very low, well under five thousand feet, and flying erratically. It failed to answer a hail, and as it approached American territory, Skull's flight leader fired a warning shot over the nose.

Except he hit the plane. The Bear abruptly banked and headed back to Russia.

Skull had thought the Russian pilot wanted to defect, not bomb L.A. or even Anchorage. He mentioned the possibility to his flight leader as they closed on the lumbering bomber. There was certainly no pressing need to fire on the plane, much less to hit it, even if the damage was probably minimal.

But his boss got a promotion out of the incident, bumped directly to general and fast-tracked at the Pentagon. He retired as a three-star muckety-muck with serious industry connections, and now worked, if you could call it that, as a consultant and lobbyist.

Hack reminded him of the Phantom commander. In some ways, the comparison wasn't fair—Preston's record showed he was a much better pilot, and undoubtedly wouldn't hit something he wanted to miss. But he had a knack for finding himself in the right place at the right time, and for making recklessness look good.

Recklessness? Was it reckless to try and pull off a major intelligence coup? If that were true, the whole mission had been reckless.

It came down to your perspective. The strike at Son Tay, the POW camp in North Vietnam, had been bold, even though it came too late to actually rescue anyone. Eagle Claw—the aborted try at rescuing the Iranian hostages under Carter—was scored by most people as idiotic, solely because of the accident at Desert 1 that doomed the mission.

And Splash?

Knowlington tapped his map, then sat back upright. He was four miles south of the airstrip. He checked the position of the helicopters carefully as he pushed northward, making damn sure to stay out their way. The last Apache, its fuel reserves pushed to the max, flittered over the ruins of the smoldering hangar and headed south. Two Chinooks followed, leaving three others and the Pave Hawks hovering in various spots over the base perimeter.

Then there was the one on the ground, sitting in front of the buildings the SAS commandos had raided. Her nose slanted into the cement, cabin crushed; smoke wicked from the side.

The Fulcrum stood astride the ramp maybe three hundred yards from the head of the runway. The wrecked Chinook was situated in such a way that the plane might not be able to squeeze past. Even if it did, the runway didn't look incredibly long; the downed chopper might make it impossible for Hack to get off.

No prisoners, no airplane. Downed helicopter, God knows how many casualties. Total wash.

That was one perspective.

Preston would come out of it okay. He had that air about him. Pentagon would want to know what the MiG looked like; he'd end up serving as some NATO liaison or something. Get his squadron command a few months after that.

He was getting that as soon as Skull got back to Home Drome.

They had given Hack a radio frequency to use to communicate with Allied planes, including Devil Flight, but it was clear when Knowlington snapped on to it. That wasn't surprising—Preston was still sitting on the ground and would have his hands full just figuring out the flight controls, let alone the radio.

"Devil Leader to Splash Delta. What's your situation?" he said, switching to the D team's com frequency.

"Devil Leader, this is Hawkins. We're about to leave with the package."

"Acknowledged. Captain, can he get around the helicopter?"

"Not sure. He's fueled. No radio, they're saying. You need details?"

"No. Okay."

As Knowlington banked south in a loose orbit parallel to the western perimeter of the base, two more Chinooks took off south. Splash Control came on to ask about his fuel situation.

"Within parameters," Knowlington responded blandly; he was actually at bingo, but had plenty of reserves to play with. Besides, it was obvious from the other traffic that he was the last available Allied air asset. Several fighters were now being scrambled to chase an Iraqi making a dash to Iran further north, and a group of Tornados had just been diverted to raid a suspected Scud site. If Preston couldn't take off, Skull was the only one close enough to smash the MiG.

He tried Hack again but got nothing. His RWR flickered with a warning. Either a GCI station far to the southeast had turned on briefly, or the equipment was just getting jittery from being north so long; in any event, the threat seemed nonexistent.

"Helis are coming out," said Splash Control, acknowledging a transmission from the Chinooks. One of the Pave Hawks hovered near the MiG, which was still sitting on the access ramp. Men were scurrying near it.

The AWACS controller warned that two more Iraqis were on the runway at an airfield further north, preparing to take off. The Tomcats would have to deal with them.

No escort for Hack.

Skull tucked back north, eyeing the obstructed runway. Takeoff distance was down to close to a thousand feet, maybe even less.

No way, Skull thought. He slipped his finger back and forth across the cannon trigger, then began a wide bank to line up his shot.

24

Hack watched the smoke pour from the rear motor of the helicopter, black furls leaking downward before dispersing sideways into a web of gray curlicues. Men were running furiously back and forth—the pilot and copilot actually seemed to have survived.

This damn close, he thought.

"Major! Major! What do you need?"

Hack jerked back around. Eugene had grabbed the flight bag and hauled it to the plane.

"My mask!" He mimed as he shouted, repeating the words. The British mechanic grabbed the mask and its hose and tossed it to him.

"The nozzle and the clamps!" Hack shouted, but Eugene had already realized he'd forgotten the adapter pieces and fished them out. Preston dropped one of the clamps, and had to wait for the mechanic to retrieve it from the ground.

He looked back at the helicopter. A fresh volley of

flames shot from the rear. An orange fist rose from the spine and smashed downward, a full body slam that shattered the metal rivets and joints.

Something tapped him on the shoulder. It was Eugene, holding the clamp.

"My board!" Hack shouted. He mimed it, and the mechanic fished it out.

Slapping it around his leg, he felt as if he was walking to the plate and someone had told him he was going to knock it out of the park.

His dad. He had this nailed.

Hack reexamined the oxygen hookup on the left panel. The modified end of his mask hose, with its flexible tubing and hand-cut nozzle face, looked and felt a little like a vacuum cleaner tool, with a metal spring clamp embedded inside. It also seemed to be about the right size without adding the second, more elaborate, plastic adapter-ring assemblies and their clamps. Hack jammed the nozzle into the receptacle on the panel and felt it click home. He pulled at it. It stayed. Oxygen flowed through. When a second jostle didn't disrupt the flow, he stowed the adapter in one of the bloodstained flaps in his pants and turned his attention to getting off the runway. With his left wrist still limp, he tried nudging the throttles with his forearm and elbow, but couldn't manage it; he had to reach across and push up the power with his right, the plane instantly jerking against her brakes, which somehow had only partially set.

Hack's right hand shook so badly as he grabbed for the stick that he tried to wrap his left hand around it to steady it before the shock of pain reminded him how badly he'd hurt it. Somehow he managed to get the brakes completely off and begin to steer the MiG down the apron, in the direction of the still-smoldering helicopter.

An Apache whipped across his path, hovering near the Chinook. The helicopter was several hundred yards away, but he was starting to move fairly quickly.

"Get out of my way!" yelled Hack. The gunship launched rockets into the hulk of the aircraft, apparently to finish off its destruction. A fireball shot from the front of the craft.

"I'm going to hit you, you asshole!" Hack shouted, but of course that didn't do any good. He reached for the brake. The Apache whipped away, and he grabbed the control stick again, his legs jelly as he slopped back and forth across the taxiway, the oscillations increasing despite his efforts to even them out.

Two modes, he remembered—the steering could be switched into a less sensitive setting.

Preston glanced down at the stick, looking briefly for the selector, but there was no way in the world he was screwing with it now. The end of the ramp was barely fifty feet ahead. He had to slide around precisely, cut the angle, and get by the rear end of the burning helicopter.

If he went off the ramp he'd sink in the sand. He steadied his feet on the rudder pedals and leaned forward to get the pit of his stomach into his elbow, glancing at the knee board as he did.

"Just do your best," he yelled at himself, and with every part of him jittering, he started the turn. The plane slid sideways as he pushed the stick and jammed at the rudder. He felt a thump, knew he was off the concrete, saw the back end of the Chinook looming on his right.

What a stinking green newbie idiotic jerkful dumbshit asshole fucked-up jackoff numbskull thing to do putting the stinking plane off the runway and losing fucking control before before before even taking off.

Numbskull. His dad used to say that.

The Fulcrum, its engines still set at seventy-percent for ground idle and its canopy still wide open, plowed across the soft earth, but kept moving. The right wing nudged one of the bent rotors of the Chinook, but cleared without damage. The MiG hopped across a cluster of potholes, and began moving cockeyed down the short strip, her nose bent slightly downward.

Clear, Hack cinched the top. It moved painfully slowly, and he cursed himself for not having closed it earlier—he couldn't afford to give up even a yard of takeoff distance.

With the top still inches from slamming home, he pitched forward on the stick as slowly and deliberately as he could, though the movement was still fairly abrupt. The nudge sent the leading edge on the tailerons downward; as they angled, he took the stick with his injured wrist and tried—impossibly—closing his knees on it, holding it as best he could as he reached his right hand to the throttle. He slid to full military power, then jammed to afterburner. The plane jerked forward, everything rushing now, the MiG veering right.

Hack grabbed the stick, holding the runway, calmer now, in control. He didn't look at the sky, or the rapidly approaching gravel at the end of the runway. He ignored everything but the speedo, got 200 km on it, then eased his control column, the front wheel slapping into the stones and dirt, a cloud of debris coming off with him as the wheels whined and the wings groaned and the plane fluttered a moment. Hack was weightless, caught in the moment when the earth and sky balanced against each other too perfectly.

Then the nose of the plane slammed upward and the MiG rammed herself forward, jumping into the air like a sprinter bolting from the blocks. Hack felt the rush of speed as the engine doors opened, the need to protect against debris gone. The plane began to buck, her nose trying to slip out of his hand—but he had it, began trimming, cleaning the airfoil, breathing regularly now through the oxygen mask, its fudged connector working without a leak, the pure air curing most of his aches and pains, even dulling the throb of his damaged wrist.

He backed the engines off, climbing steadily, in control. He checked the ladder on the HUD, took a moment to orient himself, get used to thinking in kilometers and kilograms.

Damn. Goddamn. Forty minutes from now he was going to touch down a hero.

Hot shit. Not too much of a numbskull after all.

His dad was going to be damn proud.

25

Hawkins watched with the rest from the open door of the helicopter as the MiG veered onto the runway and then raced toward the end, veering sharply upward at the last possible second and then racing away.

"Shit, yeah!" yelled Fernandez. "I knew he'd make it."

The others were laughing and cheering. Hawkins pushed back into the helicopter, where he found Wong leaning against the wall, examining a diagram of the base drawn out on one of the satellite photos.

"You pulled it off," Hawkins told his old friend. "Another medal."

Wong looked up from the map and blinked twice, an owl surprised by a searchlight in the forest. Hawkins laughed so hard he nearly lost his balance.

"What?" asked Wong.

"Nothing, Bristol." He looked back at his men, who were now settling in along the far side of the Pave Hawk. From their perspective, it had been a kick-ass mission—

one enemy base neutralized, one frontline fighter stolen.
Saddam had had his ass kicked, and his toilet paper stolen
from his stall for good measure. The D boys were all wearing smiles, trying to tell stories over the steady beat of the
MH-60's rotors.

Things weren't likely to be so lighthearted in the SAS
choppers. Miraculously, the crew in the Chinook that had
crashed had gotten out with only minor scratches. Still, the
Brits had lost two men—Sergeant Burns and one of the
paratroopers assaulting the buildings. There had been
maybe a half-dozen seriously wounded besides. More im-
portantly, the captured SAS men hadn't been found.

Two men, a helicopter. Even without the hijacking of
the MiG, the general commanding the operation would no
doubt consider the losses acceptable, given their objective.
You took care of your own.

Hawkins agreed with that. But Burns hadn't died in the
assault on the buildings. He'd been killed getting the
plane, maybe by Hawkins himself.

The plane wasn't worth a man's death. Wong himself
had said the West already knew a great deal about the
fighters. But they were all going to look like heroes,
Hawkins especially.

Fernandez said something and everyone around him,
even Eugene, laughed. As Hawkins leaned toward them to
catch what it was, Wong grabbed his arm, pulling him with
him as he leaned into the cockpit area and peered through
the front glass.

"What's up?" Hawkins yelled to him.

The Air Force intelligence officer ignored the question,
pointing back to the east and yelling at the pilot. The Pave
Hawk helicopter pilot glanced back in his direction, then
pitched the helicopter back toward the southern edge of the
base.

"What's the story, Bristol?" Hawkins yelled as Wong
slipped over to the window next to the Minimi gunner.

"The bunker area south of the base," said Wong.

"Yeah? We pinned them down but left them. They were
too far to bother us, and across a minefield."

"Why were there soldiers there?" said Wong. "Why so far from the area of importance when they could not expect an attack by land? The bunkers—what do they hold?"

He handed Hawkins the sketch he'd been examining before. Hawkins stared at the area Wong had referred to, but saw nothing.

"Bombs?"

"Too far away." He pointed. "Buzz that gully there, running south from the road. There is another bunker there."

"What?"

Wong frowned, then pushed past to talk to the pilot. Hawkins put his head to the window.

Dead Iraqis lay in the distance, slumped behind the meager defensive posts they had manned. The base lay well beyond them, the smoke now thinning.

A scratch road, no more than a trail, ran along the perimeter of the base, linking the defensive posts. It jogged south at a point parallel to the southwest corner of the airstrip, running to a small circle in front of a bunker. Calling the dug-in position a bunker was giving it a status it didn't deserve—it was more like a tarped lean-to, and a small one at that.

There were footprints in the sand near it, though, a lot of footprints. As he stared at them, Hawkins realized that there was another bunker there, this one an actual concrete structure hidden by the dirt.

Wong was right—why bother to have men there?

"The guns, man the guns!" Hawkins shouted to his team. "Yo, get your weapons. Get the fuck up! Wake up! Wake up!"

A figure popped out of the bunker on the ground, then another, and another. The .50-caliber gunner took aim.

"No," said Wong, grabbing the man. "They're surrendering. Look."

Wong was right. Six Iraqis came out of the bunker in the desert, waving white and tan shirts.

Two other figures came out behind them.

The paratroopers, who had now reversed roles with their captors. They motioned at the Iraqis, and all six of the soldiers dropped to their stomachs, hands on the backs of their heads.

"Holy shit fuck, you lucky son of a bitch," said Fernandez. Hawkins had to grab him to keep him from leaping from the helicopter. They were still a good fifty feet off the ground.

"Obviously not Republican Guards," said Wong, who seemed disappointed. "We may have to call for help to take the prisoners," he added. "There won't be room."

"I think we can manage to squeeze the bastards in," said Hawkins. "I think we can manage very well."

26

Skull had run ahead of the MiG as Hack took off, but the Mikoyan made up the distance quickly, climbing upward faster than the A-10 could go in level flight. The last of the helicopters cleared off the ground a few seconds later; Skull's job there was done.

He tracked onto the MiG's trail, intending to run behind until the backup escorts caught Hack. In the meantime, he gave the AWACS a good read on its location and direction, relaying the fact that "Splash Bird" had no radio communications.

"Devil Leader, be advised Vapor Flight has been diverted," added the controller, telling Knowlington that not only the F-14's but the backup flight of F-15C's had now been vectored north in an attempt to splash Iraqi MiGs. A pair of F-16's were being pressed into service as guard dogs for the helicopters, which were now clear of Splash and flying to the west. Coyote asked Skull to hang with Preston as long as he could. "Mirage 2000's en route, call sign Jacques. Should meet you near the border. Request you hold your present course until they arrive."

"The escort is French?"

"They speak English," snapped the controller before giving him their frequency and contact information.

Skull took down the data, then clicked into the Frenchies' circuit, but couldn't pick them up. The planes flew out of Bahrain and were still a good distance away; even optimistically, they wouldn't be within radar range for at least ten minutes.

The AWACS had alerted Allied fighters to the fact that the MiG running south was on their side. The controller assured Skull he'd broadcast updates on its position, as well as warn anything that came close. At the moment, though, Skull was the only plane even near him.

Near being extremely relative, as was evident by the controller's fix. Hack was twenty miles ahead and pulling away.

"Still climbing," said the controller.

"Thirty angels was briefed," Hack reminded Coyote. They had set thirty thousand feet for the egress to lessen the possibility of getting nailed by gunfire or pursuers, but the relatively high altitude was a problem for Skull. The Hog's engines whined just clearing fifteen thousand feet. Thirty thousand feet might very well be a world altitude record for a Hog.

Maybe Hack would bring it down a bit when he realized the pointy-noses had missed the rendezvous. Hopefully, he'd at least slow down.

Preston would be okay as a commander. He would come off as too arrogant, a bit too stuck up—but hell, after this, he'd have the bona fides. Shot down one MiG, stole another. People would line up to serve with him.

Preston would be too famous for a Warthog squadron. Hog drivers were blue-collar workers, lunch-pail guys who took the bus to work, not a limousine.

Was that what Skull would do now, take a bus to work? Where the hell would he work? What would he do?

Did he really have to resign? Should he resign? If he

never took another drink—if he never needed another drink?

Bullshit. He'd always need another drink. Always. That was a fact of life.

But what had his sister said?

"So you're going to quit?"

"I don't want to hurt these kids."

"And you wouldn't be hurting them by quitting?"

"I'm not quitting."

He was. It wasn't exactly running away, and it wasn't like there weren't plenty of other guys, plenty, who could take over for him. A lot of them could do better, even if he wasn't hitting the booze.

Maybe. Maybe not.

That was beside the point. You could *always* find someone better. And worse, for that matter.

The point was: What should he do?

Walk away. Give up.

Such a loaded phrase. Better to say retire.

Perspective again.

Maybe it was better that he hadn't bought it. He was walking away while he could still walk. He didn't have a death wish after all; that wasn't what the drinking was all about.

Somehow that seemed reassuring as he pushed the throttle for more speed, trying to catch the MiG's thinning contrail.

27

Hack backed off the throttle gingerly. He still used his right hand, though the pain had gone down quite a bit in his left; he could now manage a fair amount of pressure on the stick with it, his hands crossed awkwardly.

He flexed his left thumb as he grabbed the stick back with his right hand. The thumb itself seemed okay. Maybe that meant the injury was only a bad sprain, not a break.

As if the exact injury would make any difference at all. He put his left hand back on the stick, working like a contortionist as he reached for the HUD controls, hoping to knock down the ambient light. He had his radar on, though the selectors were unfamiliar and balky.

The F-14's still hadn't shown themselves. Granted, he was much lower than planned, only twenty thousand feet; he didn't want to go any higher with the fudged oxygen connector, though it seemed to be working fine. The radar ought to make it easier for them to find him, even if he couldn't work it well enough to find *them*.

Of course, it would also mean that other Allied aircraft could see him and possibly think he was an enemy plane.

Not if the AWACS was doing its job.

But was the radar working? The display was clean.

That couldn't be true, damn it. Did he have it on?

Hack fiddled with it some more, but finally gave up. He looked at the MiG's RWR in the bottom right-hand corner of the dash, just above his right knee. Similar to many Western units, the display was dominated by a crude outline of the aircraft. An "enemy" radar would set off the bottom row of threat lights and then touch off LEDs indicating distance, bearing, and type around the shadow of the plane in the dial.

Never in his life had Hack wished for a threat indicator to flash.

There should be a pair of F-14's. If they were tangled or diverted, two F-15's would take their place.

He wasn't sure about the Navy guys, but he knew the Air Force pilots would be smart enough to come look for him if they couldn't find him at thirty thousand feet. Surely someone had told them that he'd gotten off by now; surely the AWACS had seen him get off the ground.

Hopefully, Eugene had told them about the mask. Wong would know that was significant.

How many stinking MiGs could there be in the air anyway? On this course? Hell, they'd be all over him if he was a *real* Iraqi.

Hack laughed. He started an instrument check, looking first at the radar warning receiver. The location of the RWR was not the best, though admittedly a pilot who actually belonged in the plane wouldn't have to spend much time staring at it until necessary—as with Western models, an alarm tone would alert him that he was being scanned. Not having the proper helmet gear had deprived him of that capability, along with the radio.

He worked across the unfamiliar panel, eyes flitting back and forth because the instruments were in unfamiliar places.

Doing fine. Burning through too much fuel, maybe, but fine.

The ladder gauge on the fuel flow device was confusing as hell. He'd taken off with four thousand kilos, now had 3,800.

No. 2,800.

Had to be closer to 3,500.

Yes. No more than five hundred pounds to get into the air. They'd gone over that.

Five hundred kilos. Roughly one thousand kilos translated into a little more than fifty nautical miles of flight, with a bit of reserve. So with about 150 miles to go, he had plenty to spare.

About 150 miles? No, he was further along, much further along. He ought to be in Saudi Arabia any minute.

No. Time was compressing. He'd only just taken off.

When?

He glanced at his watch. He'd forgotten to set it when he took off.

Now *that* was a numbskull move.

Hack tapped the throttles back. The poorly designed instrument layout kept tripping him up. He had to look on the left side to get his attitude indicator, one of the most basic checks since it told him whether he was flying right side up or not. Then he had to cross back to the right to check the engines, then go up to the middle of the panel to check compass and navigation. The vertical velocity indicators were also on the right side, turning his usual across-the-board sweep into a swirling zig back and forth across the old-style instrument panel. Too many passes too quickly, he thought, and his head would be spinning.

No need for that. Just truck home. Go south, look for the big ditch, turn left fifty degrees. KKMC would be that big smudge in the center of the windscreen.

Nice if the Tomcats would show up right about now.

Hack glanced down at his knee board. The top page had notes on his contact frequencies. He didn't need them now—the radio was useless. Nor was the map on the next page of much use, nor the Western coordinates for his course, nor the notes he'd scribbled about some of the instrument settings. But he glanced at the board anyway. Just habit. Reassuring somehow.

Hack had six thousand meters on his altimeter, just over twenty thousand feet, with a forward airspeed of 675 kilometers an hour, a bit over 350 knots. He had the heading they had briefed, but he was much lower and going fifty knots faster than they had set out. He eased back on the throttle again, the plane jerking slightly as he fumbled.

If the Tomcats weren't here and the Eagles weren't here, something must have happened.

Maybe Saddam had scrambled someone to catch him.

Skull and the others would be sitting ducks in their slow-moving A-10's.

Not his problem.

They were his guys, though. He had to help them. He had the cannon, if nothing else.

Did he even have that?

The armament panel was on the right side at his elbow. Neither of his Western sources had touched on it, but Harry and he had discussed cannon shots at length before taking off a year ago.

Huge slugs. Had to slow down to use the gun. Bitch of a targeting computer. You had to get really close to fire, and hit the speed brakes if you were moving over four hundred knots.

Four hundred klicks maybe? But that was really slow, much too slow.

He did remember the procedure for arming the gun—the HUD flashed into gun mode.

Hack killed it. He had to fly on to Saudi Arabia. That was his job.

Let his guys go down?

That he couldn't do.

Hack hesitated for a moment, then pushed against the stick. It took more effort than in the F-15 to start a turn, but less than in a Hog.

28

Skull tore his eyes away from the canopy glass as the RWR began to bleat. A Slot-Back radar was looking for him twenty miles ahead, at roughly twenty thousand feet.

Either Hack had turned around, or Saddam had somehow managed to get a MiG in the air without telling anyone.

"Coyote, this is Devil One. Splash MiG has turned back in my direction."

"Coyote confirms," snapped the voice from the AWACS. It was older and sharper than before—the sergeant he'd been talking to had been replaced by the officer in charge. "What's our boy up to?"

"I believe he's looking for me," Skull said. "How are our escorts?"

"Still approaching," said Coyote.

Skull clicked back on to the French frequency and tried his hail again. This time he got a response.

"Jacques One reads you, Devil Leader," said the French

pilot, giving a position. They were a little over eighty miles away, descending from thirty thousand feet.

"I have a visual on Splash Bird. I make him twelve miles away, he's descending a little, but still around twenty thousand feet."

"Twelve miles away?"

"I eat a lot of carrots," said Knowlington. Despite the immense distance, he knew he saw the MiG.

Maybe his eyes weren't aging after all. He pushed his nose up but kept his course steady, feeling a bit like an old-fashioned commuter train chugging along as the express raced by.

So why the hell had Hack turned around? He was maybe five minutes from the border. The MiG didn't carry all that much fuel.

Probably had realized the wires were crossed on the escorts and decided to look for Skull. Without a radio he might worry that he wouldn't get clearance to land at KKMC. He'd know what he was doing fuel-wise.

Idiot was probably worried about him. Shit.

He'd have done the same thing.

"Devil Leader, Splash reports two packages aboard along with prisoners. The entire family is headed home," said the AWACS controller. "Thought you'd like to know."

"Devil Leader acknowledges," said Skull, taken by surprise.

Had they gone back and found them? Who? Wong and Hawkins and the D boys were the last to leave; he'd heard them clear the base himself.

Wong.

"Well done," added the controller.

Skull didn't respond. Congratulations always waited until you touched down and stowed your gear. That wasn't superstition; it was experience, hard-earned.

But. *But*. Hell of a way to go out. Last mission—recovered two lost SAS men, stole an Iraqi MiG.

Stole an Iraqi MiG. You couldn't top that.

Skull glanced up and saw the Mikoyan continuing toward him. Its nose rode up at a slight angle, and the wings tucked up and down, as if she were a bronco and Hack a cowboy trying to break her.

Knowlington put the Hog on her side, showing his belly to the approaching plane.

"Here I am, you son of a bitch," he said. "Come on, Hack. Let's go home."

29

Hack bounced the radar controls back and forth, trying to cajole the radar into action. He'd hit the buttons, then jerk his head back up and grab the control column, nervous about taking his attention off the sky for too long.

He ought to be able to see the Hogs, at least. And any Iraqis coming for them.

The smoke from Splash—he hoped it was Splash—filled a small finger of the hazy horizon in the lower left quadrant of his windscreen. His eyes hunted for a black stick in the mist, or a glint, or anything moving.

Turning back was dumb. He was eating up fuel.

Not according to the gauge. Three hundred kilos for takeoff, only two hundred since then. Much better than he'd expected.

And it was all flowing fine. Forget the gauge—he could hear the engines humming.

Go by time in the air, forget the tanks, he told himself.

He glanced at his watch.

Twenty-five mini-minutes after the hour.

Mini-minutes. What a joke.

Wisdom and folly, folly and wisdom. It depended on who was making the interpretation.

They were going to think he was very, very wise after this.

A black bird flapped in the sky below him, rolling its wings before belly flopping down.

One of his Hogs.

About time. Hack banked, turning the MiG back toward Saudi Arabia. She had a tight turn—he could feel the g's popping him in the chest, even with the suit.

Too bad for the Iraqi pilot. Might have been interesting if they had captured him alive, gotten him to talk to them.

Hack hadn't been thinking of that in the hangar. Wong had mentioned it as a possibility before.

Wong. What a character.

Hack glanced at his watch. It was still 7:25 A.M. Had it stopped?

No. Time was just moving very slowly. He must not be having any fun.

His left arm jerked upward, the wrist and forearm muscles spasming. Hack stared at them as if they belonged to a creature that had somehow invaded the cockpit from a cheap sci-fi movie. Finally he put his hand back down on the throttle, slowly palming the thick lever.

Time to go home. His legs and arms and head were heavy as hell.

So were his eyes.

Jesus, he was tired. Normally Hack carried a small packet of amphetamines in one of his small flap pockets. While he loathed using them, had never in fact used them, he reached down now, afraid he wouldn't be quite up to the demanding task of landing the unfamiliar plane.

He tapped his fingers against his leg, then felt a wave of disorienting panic—the pocket with the pills wasn't there.

He'd forgotten he was wearing the Iraqi gear.

The Hog was on his right, climbing through maybe fif-

teen thousand feet, struggling to reach his altitude. Hogs
were great at everything except climbing.

The MiG jerked sharply to the left, plunging downward
as its wing tipped toward the ground. Hack's head floated
somewhere above his body as warning lights flashed; as
his lungs gasped, he stared at the dials, unsure of what had
happened.

Fuel. He was out of fuel.

Fuel?

No, the RPM gauge showed the left engine had stopped
working.

Hack struggled to clear his head, struggled simply to
breathe. His hands worked on their own, stabilizing the
MiG as it fell through sixteen thousand feet, grabbing it by
its bootstraps.

Restart, he told himself. Go.

His brain was stuck in a block of plastic, unable to communicate with the rest of his body.

The fuel flow. What was the stinking gauge saying?

Why was he so concerned with fuel? He had plenty—
just go for the start.

The engine rumbled, seemingly on its own. Hack tried
to calm his breathing, pulling the MiG back level. Knowlington had swooped on his right, trying to close up the distance. Hack gave him a thumbs-up, but was too busy to try
any other hand signals.

Both of his briefers had said the Mikoyan never flamed
out, and if it did, it would be easy to keep from spinning.

Easy for them to say.

Forget that. Both power plants were working now.

He'd been doing nothing that should have given the engines trouble. More than likely, the problem was a result
of crappy Iraqi maintenance, not his flying—but that was
hardly very reassuring. Hack gingerly pulled back on the
control column, leveling off at 4,500 meters, roughly fifteen thousand feet.

Fifteen thousand white-robed angels, fluttering in the
sky.

He glanced at the yellow handles beneath his leg. The

seat would save him, but damn, no way he was going out now. Not this close. They couldn't be two minutes from the border.

The RWR lights blinked on.

Two contacts, on his left wing. The lights' colors would have given him more information, but he couldn't remember the code.

Had to be friendlies. Where the hell was his Hog?

On his right, maybe a hundred yards away. Knowlington.

It would be Knowlington, that son of a bitch. He was an alky in D.C., but here, damn it, here he was a hero. Couldn't ask for a better commander or a wing mate.

Jesus, his head hurt. He blew a wad of air into his mask. Sky was dark.

Fifteen thousand feet. Damn low, lowest he'd ever flown.

High for a Hog driver.

His head felt too light. The amphetamine had kicked in.

He hadn't taken the amphetamine.

Oxygen, numbskull, there's a problem with the oxygen. You're hyperventilating CO_2.

30

Skull pushed his nose level as Hack knifed downward on his left wing, slinging the MiG nearly parallel to him. It was a nice piece of flying, actually, though for a moment it seemed as if the MiG's engines had flamed, the plane stuttering in the sky.

"Jacques One to Devil Flight, we are advised that you and your friend are now on course."

"Devil One. Affirmative. You still don't have us on radar?"

"Negative," said the Frenchman, whose accent sounded slightly English, not French. In any event, his voice was clear and crisp. "We should be within radar range shortly."

The French warplanes were equipped with a pulse-Doppler unit that was supposed to be able to pick up targets from outside fifty miles. But the specs were proving too optimistic; the AWACS commander told Skull they were now within forty miles, and he should correct due south five degrees if possible to complete their intercept.

"Hang with me, Hack," said Skull, turning to eye his silent wingman. He waved again, trying to signal the course adjustment and that the Mirages were ahead, but Preston's eyes remained fixed dead ahead.

"Won't be long now," he said, checking his position against the map. He made it five minutes to the border.

The MiG spurted ahead as Skull made his adjustment. Coyote asked for a situation report, and Skull told him they were still looking for the Mirages.

"You have clear skies to Emerald City," said the supervisor, sounding jaunty—or at least jaunty for an AWACS controller. This was one mission no one was going to forget. "How's his fuel?"

"No way of knowing," said Skull. "Maybe tight, maybe not."

"You're over Saudi territory. Anything happens and he wants to bail, he's safe," said Coyote. "Half the Air Force'll be there to grab him."

"Thanks."

"Affirmative."

No way Hack was going to bail now, thought Skull. He pushed his throttle, trying to keep up.

31

The MiG's altimeter pegged 4,800 kilometers. He'd never gone over 6,500 klicks, which was about twenty thousand. Too low to suffer decompression problems.

In theory. But when Hack's eyes found the panel, he saw that not only wasn't his oxygen hose snugged, it wasn't in at all. He'd pulled it out at some point, probably twisting his arms across his body. He'd been hyperventilating for God knows how long. No wonder he thought everything was a joke.

Preston reached over to the panel, angry that he had let himself get tripped up by something so simple. He shouldn't even need oxygen here. This was a Sunday drive. All he had to do was breathe slow and easy.

His wrist gave way as he touched the nozzle end, and he shrieked with pain. He pushed back in the seat, gathered himself, made sure the MiG was flying all right, did his instrument check. Then he reached across to push the nozzle in with his right hand.

The left engine picked that moment to quit again. And this time, the right engine joined it.

Hack slammed the tube adapter home, then grabbed the stick, pulling back in an attempt to stop the MiG from entering a dive. He realized he'd pulled too hard, and he eased off. Two full, clean breaths of pure oxygen, and the black cellophane that had been slowly strangling him melted away.

Hack began working the restart procedure, fingers fumbling against the panel on the right side of the cockpit as he tried to hold the control column with his left hand. But the buffeting against the hydraulic controls was too much for his injured wrist, and the plane jerked from his weakened fingers. He grabbed for the stick with his right hand; as he did so, his eyes went to the fuel gauge, and he realized that he had been misreading the indicators.

The engines hadn't stalled. They'd run out of fuel. The flow seemed to be restricted somehow, but at this point he no longer trusted the indicators or his ability to read the gauges.

And in any event, it was rapidly becoming academic.

The plane yawed left, fighting the stick. He was losing altitude fast. He had to keep his hand on the stick, get the plane stable, then play with the fuel selectors and try to restart.

Glide, you son of a bitch. Glide.

He got the wings even, got the nose almost level. He gave a push against the stick, nudged his left elbow there, holding the plane as he went back to try and restart.

Too much to do with only one good arm.

Out, out, I have to get out.

Out.

Fuck that. Not now.

Restart. There had to be fuel in the damn thing. Switch the tanks. Get into the sumps.

You're not flying a Hog.

Out! Out! Level the wings and out.

Just out!

His body seemed to spin from inside his spine. His

stomach pushed out through the flight suit, past the restraints. His left hand screamed with pain and his legs
slammed against the seat.

The handle, pull the handle.

He already had. The canopy failed to clear. Hack shot
through it, propelled like a human cannonball from the
plane as it turned upside down.

An ax pounded on his head. Something smashed his
legs—a safety cable activated by the ejection system,
keeping them close to the seat as he went out.

Black ice spun around his head. Fire pressed against his
chest and legs. Hack sped toward the ground faster than
the speed of sound, yanking around as the seat did its
magic, the world a complete blurry rush. He remembered
his father, saw him now smiling at him when he was nine,
a Little League game.

"Hey, Dad, I hit a home run. I hit a home run."

The parachute jerked open.

And then the strap from the Iraqi pilot's suit, which had
been ever so slightly torn by the shrapnel from the grenade
that killed its owner, gave way.

32

The crash happened so quickly that Skull didn't realize what was going on until the MiG started to spin.

The way he saw it, the way he would tell it to the investigators later, both engines must have quit at the same time. The plane edged down, then one of the power plants recaught, hard, exploding as if the afterburner suddenly slammed on, and the plane went into an uncontrollable yaw.

Until that moment, Hack had probably figured he could control it. That was the kind of guy he was—he didn't give up, and he was cocky enough to figure he could work himself out of any jam.

But even he had his limits. He went for the handles. The canopy didn't come off, but the seat sure came out, flying out almost straight down. Skull started to bank, keeping one eye on the MiG, which was now pirouetting not fifty yards from him. He saw, or thought he saw, the chute open. Then there was debris in the air, or he thought he saw debris, or just sensed there was something—the chute disappeared and he pulled up on his stick, trying to stay clear.

He circled back, dropping low and slow. By that time, the parachute was skittering along the ground, crazy-curled by the wind. He spotted the seat, and then saw Preston, who ought to have released the chute, who ought to have been standing there, probably kicking the desert because he had been so goddamn close, so stinking damn close, to hitting a grand slam, landing an Iraqi MiG back on a U.S. base for all the world to see.

But he wasn't. He was lying in the sand, his body crumpled. It didn't take more than a single pass to know he was dead.

Epilogue

HANGING AROUND

1

No way in the world was it possible to debrief a mission—to even *think* about a mission—without coffee. Hell, it was against Air Force regulations and probably the U.S. Constitution to even try that. The Geneva Convention most likely declared it punishable by hanging, and the UN undoubtedly had a commission on it.

So as soon as Shotgun touched down at the Home Drome, right after he parked and popped the hood and plopped down on the tarmac next to Sergeant Rosen, who was taking personal care of his aircraft this morning, right after he gave the rest of the crew a quick thumbs-up and pointed to the slew of holes in the airframe—unnecessary, actually, due to the rather obvious gashes and dripping fluids—and after giving the appropriate shrug to an airman's "You actually managed to get home like that?" Shotgun ambled over to the only place at King Fahd that could be relied upon for A-1 Debriefing Strength Joe—his quarters.

Regrettably, Shotgun had not yet completed his plans to rig his commercial Bunn to an IFF device, which would allow the unit to begin grinding and brewing as his Hog approached the runway. He therefore had to wait an excruciating ninety seconds while the machine processed a choice selection of hand-picked African and Colombian beans and then dripped distilled mountain water into the pot.

The interlude gave him time to contemplate a philosophical question: What should he have for breakfast, Friehoffer's or Entenmann's?

Technically, neither of the famed Northeast bakeries was listed among the official military suppliers providing food at the mess. But Shotgun had a direct line to outlet stores for both, and with the help of several well-connected supply sergeants—there were no other kind of supply sergeants, after all—he had managed to schedule regular deliveries from both. In fact, a C-5A with a fresh load of cheese strudel and sticky buns ought to be due at any moment. Still undecided between the bakeries, he filled his thirty-ounce ceramic coffee mug and left the tent.

Shotgun had walked about two sips' worth toward the unloading area when Billy Bozzone flagged him down.

"Coffee's in my tent," he told Bozzone, a lieutenant who had grown up on Staten Island but was otherwise a good sort. "Goin' over to grab some Entenmann's, I think. Or maybe Friehoffer's. Kind of waiting for inspiration to strike."

"Intel guys are looking for you," said Bozzone. "Delta major too."

"Yeah, I'm on my way," said Shotgun. "What's the rush?"

"You haven't heard? Preston's dead. MiG malfunctioned and he fell out of the parachute harness."

For the first time since he came to the Gulf, Shotgun could find nothing to say.

2

Sergeant Rosen's fingers betrayed her, fumbling everything from screws to cables, even slipping off the controls
of an oscilloscope. She couldn't staunch the adrenaline,
couldn't slow the thump of her heart as she worked.

Was BJ all right? What had happened north? Where the
hell was he?

Every comment from someone in Oz threw her. Every
roar of a jet or whistle of landing gear took her attention
away from what she was doing. Finally, after nearly
smashing a screwdriver through the radar unit in Shotgun's
plane, she put down her tools and began walking away.

"Sarge, what's up?" called one of the crew.

"Gotta leak," she told him mildly.

"You selling tickets?"

"You won't make enough money in three lifetimes,
Tommy," she said. "Put that unit back together for me,
will ya?"

"Gotcha, Sarge."

Her legs began to shake as she walked toward the small rest room stall in the back of one of Oz's hangars. By the time she pushed the door closed behind her, her knees were jelly. As she sat on the commode, her hands began to shake and she realized she was crying.

I can't do this, she told herself. There's no way I can do this.

Joining the military didn't mean you had to give up being human. Nor did it mean that you had to stow your emotions.

But.

But.

Rebecca Rosen felt as if she'd slipped into someone else's body. The limbs didn't work quite the same way. The head seemed at a permanent tilt, and the borrowed eyes made the light seem more yellow.

No. This wasn't her. She wouldn't do it. She couldn't.

Feet scuffled along the floor a few yards away. Sergeant Rosen ran her fingers through her short hair and pinched down the skin behind her ears. She took a long breath, reached around, and flushed the commode.

Outside, she scowled when a staff sergeant said something about Shotgun's plane needing an entire overhaul, new sumps, new fuel system, new skin.

"No fuckin' way," she said. "Just go get Tinman. He'll tell you what to do if you can't handle it."

"Sump's shot out," said the sergeant.

"You want me to fuckin' kiss it and make it better?"

The sergeant scurried back under the plane.

"Getting on them kind of hard this morning, no?" growled Sergeant Clyston from behind her.

"There's no fucking way we're losing an airplane because it has a couple of dents," Rosen told him. "It can be fixed. I checked it myself."

Clyston nodded, but said nothing.

A half hour later, Lieutenant Dixon and Gunny landed. By then, details of the mission had spread through Oz. Rosen and the others knew that the SAS men had been rescued and the MiG stolen. They also knew that Dixon's radio had been shot out—and that Major Preston had been killed when the MiG malfunctioned and he had to bail.

Sergeant Rosen stayed back in the hangars when Dixon landed. With any other pilot, on any other day, she would have among the first to inspect the plane. Instead, she busied herself with a balky INS unit on a bench at the furthest end of Devil Squadron Hangar 1.

Still, her hands trembled when she heard his voice behind her. Still, her heart seemed to stop when he touched her shoulder gently.

She let herself step back into the borrowed body for a brief moment, turning and hugging him. It was a warm hug, and even though the world sat at a slant, even though the light seemed all wrong, there was a certain comfort— maybe a great comfort.

"Gotta work," she said, pushing away sharply, regaining herself. "Gotta get this done ASAP. Sorry."

Silent, Dixon stood watching her. How long he stood there, she couldn't say, but she knew when she turned that he would be gone, and he was.

3

"You did a goddamn good job," the general told Skull after he picked up the phone in his office. "You hit a grand slam."

Knowlington pulled out his chair and sat down as the general continued. The British were ecstatic, the Delta people were ecstatic, even the CinC, the man himself, was ecstatic.

They all knew that he'd lost a pilot. They weren't being insensitive; they were putting it in perspective.

Actually, they *were* being insensitive, but that was the way it was. Skull would have expected no less if he had bought it and Preston had managed to get the MiG back to the base intact.

He'd circled the wreck while the SAR people came in. The pararescuers told him Preston had been ripped from the parachute by the force of the ejection. The Iraqi gear had been damaged somehow; one of the clasps had come loose or the strap ripped or both. A freak accident, a one-in-a-million shot.

"Just unlucky," said the pararescuer. "Stinking damn unlucky."

The plane had crashed in the desert about a mile away. It was bent but mostly there. A team had already secured it for transport. There had been no fire. Wong, who was en route to the scene, suspected that the plane's fuel system or gauges had malfunctioned and the tanks had run bone-dry.

Maybe one of the gauges on the dash had malfunctioned, or maybe Hack had miscalculated by using the afterburners, or maybe they'd made a mistake on the ground when they loaded the fuel in. Any of those things could have happened. Maybe all of them had.

Even so, it shouldn't have been fatal. Worst case, Hack should have been able to float down to earth, cursing the whole way.

A freak, unlucky thing.

There'd be a thick report circulated around the Pentagon and Congress and even the White House.

"Preston deserves a medal," said the general.

"Absolutely," said Skull.

"We want that in high gear. We may go for the big one. I think it's worth it. Risked his life under fire. Honor for us all."

"Okay," said Knowlington.

The line went silent for a moment. "Preston wasn't a friend of yours, was he?"

"Hated my guts, I think," said Skull.

"Word is he wanted your job."

"Wouldn't want a DO who didn't."

"We'll get you a replacement. Say, Mike, did you call to give me a back door on the mission, or was something else up?"

To quit, to walk away—it would be like leaving a job half done. It would be like letting down his guys, his kids, his boys.

Damn, he wanted a drink. He wanted it so bad his tongue burned and he could feel anger rising inside. He

wanted it so bad he felt like yelling into the phone, screaming, "I just lost a goddamn pilot. And why? Why? Because
grabbing a plane out from Saddam's nose was just too cool
a thing to pass up, because I felt sorry for myself and
wanted to go out in a blaze of glory, because Hack wanted
my job and figured he could get it by pulling off the impossible, because of some freak, absurd accident."

Because that's the way war was.

He wanted a drink, and somehow that was enough to
make him stay.

"Yeah, I called to tip you off," Skull told the general. "I
knew you'd want to be in the loop."

"I appreciate it, Mikey. Commendation in this for you
too. Maybe a medal. Definitely a medal. Have to be. Air
Force Cross. God, what'll that be? Your third?"

If he'd had just a little more strength, or been a little less
tired, or needed a drink a little less badly, Skull might have
told the general what he could do with the medal. Instead
he just hung up the phone.

A Note to Readers

While "suggested" by an actual operating area near the front line, Ar Kehy is an invention, as is the Iraqi base. As usual, I played around with some of the architecture and furniture of the historical places mentioned in the book.

RAF Tornados served with great distinction in a variety of roles during the Gulf War. Sister Sadie and her crew, of course, are fictitious, though the advanced near-real-time reconnaissance systems described in the book are not.

British SAS operations are covered by the Official Secrets Act, but there have nonetheless been some interesting and detailed reports about British goings-on in Iraq. Among the most entertaining is Andy McNab's *Bravo Two Zero*, which was published in America in 1994 by Island Books.

Some specific details relating to actual combat operations or procedures that could conceivably aid an enemy during war have been omitted or obscured. Some details covering special operations, intelligence, and technical information-gathering processes have been slightly altered. The changes haven't materially affected the tale.

I'd like to thank my editor, Tom Colgan, as well as Samantha Mandor and all the other people at Berkley who have helped bring these books to you. Thanks also to Jake

Elwell at Wieser & Wieser. Check six, and whatever you do, don't spill the coffee.

   —Ferro
   Thrllrdad@aol.com

SOMETHING EXPLODED IN THE SKY...

...something metallic, something swirling, something from hell. Four dark beasts filled the southeastern horizon like the lions of the Apocalypse. The reflection of morning light off the sand splayed like blood across their wings...

HOGS: GOING DEEP
by James Ferro

___0-425-16856-5/$5.99

Also Available:

Hogs #2: Hog Down   0-425-17039-X/$5.99

Hogs #3: Fort Apache 0-425-17306-2/$5.99

Hogs #4: Snake Eaters 0-425-17815-3/$5.99

Hogs #5: Target Saddam 0-425-18073-5/$5.99

TOM CLANCY

with General Carl Stiner (Ret.)

Shadow

Inside the Special Forces

Warriors

PUTNAM